"I don't want to want you."

He accompanied the admission with a sweeping caress of her nipple.

Electricity sizzled in her veins, the sparks echoing in her head.

"You're everything I told myself I shouldn't have. Everything that's destructive to me. And yet—" he cupped her, levered up and sucked her into his mouth, his tongue licking and circling her flesh before crushing a kiss to her lips "—you've become my fantasy."

"And you hate us both for it," she whispered against his lips.

He stared at her, his wolf eyes so bright, so intense they almost hurt to look into.

"Yes. Almost."

A sharp pain ~~carved into her~~ honed by the tender to hate him back, to care. This was sex more.

But her ach

Secrets of a One Night Stand by Naima Simone is part of the Billionaires of Boston series.

Dear Reader,

I am a fairy-tale-retellings junkie. I love to read them, and I adore writing them. And the moment Achilles Farrell appeared in his brother Cain's story, I knew he would be the Beast and it would be my pleasure to find him the perfect Beauty.

Wounded, guarded Achilles is the middle brother, branded by the Boston media as the Feral Farrell. He's just biding his time until he fulfills the terms of his biological father's will and then he can return to his secluded home in the mountains of Washington State. But he doesn't count on meeting a beautiful, mysterious woman in a local dive bar and having a hot one-night stand with her. Definitely doesn't plan on running into that woman again months later when she applies for a job with his family's company. She's a part of the world he detests, the world he's running from. But he can't run fast or far enough from her. And he finds that he might not want to...

I hope you fall in love with Achilles and Mycah in *Secrets of a One Night Stand*!

Happy reading!

Naima

NAIMA SIMONE

SECRETS OF A ONE NIGHT STAND

HARLEQUIN
DESIRE

DESIRE™

ISBN-13: 978-1-335-73511-9

Secrets of a One Night Stand

Harlequin Enterprises ULC
22 Adelaide St. West, 40th Floor
Toronto, Ontario M5H 4E3, Canada
www.Harlequin.com

Printed in U.S.A.

USA TODAY bestselling author **Naima Simone**'s love of romance was first stirred by Harlequin books pilfered from her grandmother. Now she spends her days writing sizzling romances with a touch of humor and snark.

She is wife to her own real-life superhero and mother to two awesome kids. They live in perfect domestically challenged bliss in the southern United States.

Books by Naima Simone

Harlequin Desire

Back in the Texan's Bed
Ruthless Pride

Billionaires of Boston

Vows in Name Only
Secrets of a One Night Stand

Blackout Billionaires

The Billionaire's Bargain
Black Tie Billionaire
Blame It on the Billionaire

HQN Books

The Road to Rose Bend

Visit the Author Profile page at Harlequin.com, or naimasimone.com, for more titles.

You can also find Naima Simone on Facebook, along with other Harlequin Desire authors, at Facebook.com/HarlequinDesireAuthors!

To Gary. 143.

One

Achilles Farrell had been called many things in his thirty years.

Dumb fuck.

Ex-con.

Bastard.

That last one behind his back since most people were leery of insulting a six-foot-four-inch-tall, 214-pound man to his face.

But never had he been called an heir.

Brother.

And in the space of one afternoon, he'd become both.

After a shock like that, he needed alcohol. Lots of alcohol.

Achilles stared at the neon red signs advertising the various beers on tap as well as framed posters declaring this pub the best *and* worst Beacon Hill, Massachusetts, had to offer. Hopefully, that ambiguity didn't translate to its liquor quality.

It'd been a couple of hours, but he could still feel the judgmental gazes of "polite" Boston society on his skin like a thousand ants. The sensation deepened his thirst for the coffee-and-caramel flavor of a perfectly drawn Guinness, sharpened his anticipation for the burn of whiskey down his throat. Had him damn near demanding the bartender bring him another round when he hadn't even requested his first drink yet.

"What can I get you?" The bartender leaned on the scarred bar top. Despite the colorful tattoos running the length of both arms, the young woman barely looked old enough to drink the alcohol she was serving.

"A shot of Jameson and a Guinness."

She nodded. "Coming up."

Only when she turned around to start building his drink did he exhale, some of the tension in his shoulders leaking out of him like a slowly released valve. Maybe once that Irish whiskey hit the back of his throat, the cold in his bones from that mockery of a funeral would finally dissipate.

To think, just three days ago, he'd been in his small cabin, alone except for his computers, just the way he liked it. That's when he'd received a certified letter about the death of a man his mother had always refused to talk about although she'd given Achilles his last name. Achilles hadn't given a damn then, just like he didn't now, about a will or an inheritance. But morbid curiosity about the man who'd impregnated his mother had compelled him to accept the paid-for plane ticket and travel thousands of miles across the country.

As soon as he'd stepped off the plane and met the glacial expression of the chauffeur, Achilles had regretted his rash decision. He'd thought landing in prison had cured him of his hot, impulsive behavior. Apparently not. And now he was paying for his spur-of-the-moment decision to attend the funeral and the reading of the will for his so-called father.

A year.

He had to give up an entire year of his life, remain in Boston, with half brothers he didn't know, and run a company he had no clue how to operate. A company he wanted no part of.

That was the price his father demanded Achilles remit.

Even from the grave, Barron Farrell was a selfish, narcissistic asshole.

When he was growing up, Achilles had begged his mother to tell him who his father was, to introduce Achilles to him. She'd always refused both requests. He'd resented her then. If she were alive, he'd thank her.

He propped his elbows on the bar top and ground his thumb and forefinger into his eyes. What he wouldn't give to be back in Tacoma, Washington, in his cabin less than a mile from the Cascade Range. So far away from affluent Beacon Hill, Massachusetts. And not just in location.

Yeah, Tacoma had its wealthy, but as the son of a

waitress, he didn't have any use for them. In his experience, the rich either fucked you or fucked you over.

But as he'd stood in that mansion's ridiculously huge library with its hardwood floor, leather furniture, fireplaces large enough for even him to stand in, spiral staircase and floor-to-ceiling bookshelves, it hadn't been just his black thermal shirt, faded jeans and battered brown boots that had differentiated him from the other men in the room.

Cain Farrell—his older brother, the heir, the son Barron Farrell had kept and acknowledged. Kenan Rhodes—the youngest son, biracial and the other bastard besides Achilles. But both men hailed from the same world. Boston's elite. It was in the razor-sharp yet elegant cut of their suits. The cultured speech. The arrogant demeanor.

Achilles had encountered people like them. And had ended up despising every one of them.

Now he had to call them brother.

Life should really offer him a cigarette when it decided to fuck him.

Again.

"You starting a tab or paying for these now?" The bartender set a mug filled with dark, cold brew topped with a creamy head that spilled a little over the rim. Next to it sat a short, smooth glass of amber whiskey.

Perfect.

"A tab." Because yeah, he was just getting started. The whole purpose of this trip entailed not thinking. And several rounds should accomplish his mission.

"I'll be back, then."

She cocked her head, running a dark blue gaze down his frame. He'd hit six foot his sophomore year of high school and had kept growing. He'd become used to that glint in a woman's eyes. And he didn't shy from it. The only thing better than losing himself in alcohol was hot, dirty, nameless sex.

His height, his build and his eyes—those were the only things his worthless sperm donor had passed down to him, and women seemed to eat that shit up. He picked up the shot of Jameson and knocked it back, never breaking visual contact with the pretty brunette. The corner of her lips lifted, desire flickering in her gaze as it dipped to his mouth.

"Let me know if you need to order food. Y'know, to balance all that alcohol. Can't have you too wasted just in case you have later…plans." She smirked before sauntering off to the other end of the bar.

"Hmm. That was subtle."

Achilles stiffened.

That voice.

Like a fire beating back the coldest winter winds.

Like fingernails on a chalkboard.

As silken and sexy as skin sliding over bare, heated skin.

As jarring as crashing cymbals directly in the ear.

He longed to curl up against it, roll around in it.

He wanted to snarl at it, hurl himself away from it.

His heart smashed against his rib cage like a caged beast. His pulse, in sharp contrast, a sonorous warning at the base of his throat. Something primitive inside him warned that he should go find that bartender with the invitation in her eyes, pay for his drinks and get the hell out.

But the impulsive, destructive streak that had brought him to Massachusetts must have still been alive and kicking because he didn't heed that warning. Instead, he slowly turned around on his barstool.

Jesus Christ.

That sense of self-preservation had been right.

This woman was everything he usually avoided.

Gorgeous. Pampered. Rich. He didn't need to see the price tag on the purple pantsuit that conformed to her abundant, wicked curves to know it cost more than everything he'd packed in his suitcase back at the hotel. Including the luggage.

A Trojan horse.

That's what she was.

Designed to appear like one thing—something innocuous—while inside was a virus waiting to strike, to infect…to destroy.

He dealt with those deadly viral strands during his job as a software developer. He'd suffered the poison of one after tangling with a woman like her.

Her dark gaze slid over him, and—in spite of knowing who she was, what she was—his breath snagged on the ragged resentment in his chest. Blood heated in his veins…pounded in his lengthening dick.

Apparently, his cock could give two damns what tax bracket she fell in.

She lifted a slim hand, hailing the bartender over to her. And in the magical way her kind had, the bartender abandoned the person she was talking to and headed their way.

Flicking a glance over Achilles, the brunette hiked her chin at the woman next to him. "What can I get you?"

"I'll have…" She narrowed her eyes, tapping a pale pink–painted finger against her tad-too-full bottom lip. "I'll have the bacon cheeseburger with a side of onion rings. Make that an extra-large order. And a Budweiser."

Well…damn.

As if she'd heard the astonished words in his head, she arched a dark eyebrow.

"They have wonderful hamburgers here and the best onion rings in Boston." She dipped her head in the direction of the bartender, who disappeared through a swinging door on the other side of the bar. "She was right, you know. You might want some food. I recommend one of the burgers or the fish 'n' chips. Make sure you're sober enough for—" the barest hint of a smirk whispered over a corner of her mouth "—later."

Was she flirting? If so, teasing him about fueling up to fuck another woman had to be one of the weirdest come-ons…or the hottest. Possibly both.

His dick twitched as she flicked a tight, honey-brown curl away from her cheek.

Definitely both.

Disgust for himself trickled through him, and he picked up his Guinness, gulping the sweet and bitter ale until nearly half of it disappeared before he settled the glass mug back on the bar top. But the cold alcohol did nothing to douse the flickers of lust in his gut.

Not when wisps of her scent—an earthy musk carrying hints of lavender, cedar and something more elusive—drifted to him, taunting him. Not when a glance down ensnared him in the dichotomy of a lush thigh and a delicate ankle. One invited his hungry teeth and the other his gentle fingers.

He had no business being tempted by either.

Women like her... They only wanted one thing from men like him. And while he didn't mind a night of hot, no-strings sex, it was being looked at like trash afterward that didn't work for him. Being someone's dirty secret tainted the soul, and that kind of stain was hell washing out.

She sighed, and out of the corner of his eye, he caught her folding a napkin until it formed a tiny square.

"I'm sorry. I didn't mean to be so flippant or rude." She broke off as the bartender reappeared and set her beer in front of her, removing the cap.

The woman smiled at her in thanks, and Achilles glanced away as another bolt of lust speared him in the chest. And lower. A dimple. Of fucking course. Because cheekbones as sharp as broken glass, eyes the color of melted dark chocolate, a mouth a shade too wide and a sinner's prayer past too full weren't enough. Because tight, springy curls the shade of sun-warmed honey wasn't overkill. She needed dimples.

"I'm usually not so forward. I'm blaming it on jet lag." She shook her head, picking up her beer and raising it to her lips.

And by all that was holy, he should've looked away.

Shouldn't have stared so openly, so…so eagerly at how that beautiful mouth pursed around the opening. Or how her delicate throat worked as she swallowed. His fingers tightened around the handle of his mug. Either that or do something that would get him booted out of the bar and possibly arrested. Like lean forward and wrap his hand around that elegant throat so he could feel every swallow against his palm. Feel the vibration of that husky contralto when she spoke.

He fixed his gaze on the rest of the ale in his glass. "Jet-lagged from where?"

He didn't glimpse her surprise, but it crackled over him just the same. As did her soft delight when she said, "London. I was there on business, and you'd think after being away from home for a week the first thing I'd want to see is my own bed, but I can't go—" She broke off, and Achilles glanced at her. But she didn't continue the sentence, instead taking another sip, then setting the bottle on the bar, studying the dark brown glass with a small frown. But her expression cleared as she looked at him. "Anyway, I found myself craving a greasy burger and a beer from my favorite bar."

As someone who'd learned early in life that detecting a lie could save him from being backhanded by whomever his mom happened to be dating, he could sense an untruth when he heard it.

"You sat down by me," he said.

She nodded. "I did."

"You started talking to me."

The corner of her mouth twitched because the "uninvited" went unspoken but might as well as have been shouted to the ceiling. "True."

"And you're never going to see me again after tonight."

"Also true."

"So you don't have to bother with bullshit. Either you tell me the truth or tell me you don't want to get into it. But don't lie."

She stared at him, pretty lips parted. She wasn't the only one surprised. He lived and worked alone for a reason: he didn't really care for people. Liked talking to them even less. Developing computer software encompassed designing algorithms, producing code, testing applications and troubleshooting existing systems. Challenging, but it came down to numbers, to science.

Not emotions. Not baggage. Not history. Not on which side of the tracks a person resided.

People were messy as fuck and he wanted no part of them.

Which didn't explain why he'd decided to engage Ms. Beacon Hill in conversation.

That dimple flashed again as her lips slowly curved into a smile that had his chest seizing and his dick hardening.

"You're right. There's something to be said for the gift of having only the 'right now,' isn't there? It's temporary, which somehow makes it more special, exciting." She extended her hand toward him. "Mycah."

After a brief hesitation, Achilles accepted that slim, smaller hand in his own. And exhaled a low, long breath when his completely encompassed hers. "Achilles."

"Achilles," she repeated, and he clenched his jaw when she emitted a little hum afterward, as if savoring his name on her tongue and finding it satisfying. "I like that name. Well, Achilles." She picked up her beer bottle once more and tipped it toward him in a toast. "Here's to strangers meeting for a night."

He lifted his mug, tapping it to her beer. And he couldn't prevent his rebellious gaze from traveling down the graceful column of her neck, past her slim shoulders to a pair of beautiful breasts that might not fill his hands but would damn sure make their presence known. Her open suit jacket offered him an unhindered view of high-waisted pants and a slightly rounded belly that he found sexy as hell. A woman who ordered the kind of meal she had, who didn't starve herself...

He shifted his scrutiny to her face of contrasting angles and curves and narrowed his eyes, studying her anew. Her clothes, those shoes with their red bottoms that even a fashion idiot like him recognized, her flawless makeup and smooth, pampered, almond-brown skin—all of that shouted wealth.

But the decadence of her food order, the roundness of her stomach, the gorgeous lushness of curves that society dictated she diet away, even her laid-back choice in beer and bar... Those all pointed to a woman who indulged herself. A woman who knew restraint but also understood that abandon wasn't always the opposite of losing control.

What would it be like to have this woman lose control all over him?

"To strangers and one night."

As they sipped their respective drinks, and the Guinness flowed over his tongue and down his throat, he couldn't shake the sense that his words had never been more prophetic.

Good thing he didn't believe in that shit.

Two

"Team Dean or Team Sam?"

Achilles lifted his mug of Guinness to his mouth, and for some odd reason Mycah Hill found herself studying the length and width of his fingers. Before she'd entered her favorite Beacon Hill bar tonight, she'd always considered herself a shoulders-and-arms woman. God knew, Achilles had that covered, as well. Massive. That black thermal cotton showed off the wide, tight, big perfection of both.

But his *fingers*.

She'd never been so fascinated by the proportion, length and...elegance of a man's fingers. Until tonight.

"Dean." His answer snatched her from her inspection of his blunt-tipped fingernails. "Natural-born leader and selfless. Let me guess." He arched a dark, thick eyebrow. "Sam."

She scoffed. "That wasn't the least bit condescending."

He stared at her.

"Oh, so what?" she snapped. "Sam was resilient, and he had a lot of obstacles to overcome. Being half demon. Losing his soul. And through it all he learned discipline, had to work through guilt and remorse and learn to forgive himself. Plus, he was self-sacrificing."

"You loved his abs."

"They were straight out of the God's Handiwork Supermart, aisle eight."

Oh, wow. The corner of that deliciously carnal mouth twitched. All night, images of his face wreathed in a full-out smile had fluttered through her head. And all night, she'd hungered to see one. That desire hadn't been fulfilled. Yet each quirk of his lips like the one she'd just been given lit her up. Ridiculous, considering they'd just met, and she didn't know him and wouldn't see him again after they both left this bar, but still...

A gift.

It'd taken greasy bar food, a couple of rounds of drinks and several rounds of "Who's better?" to break the sheet of ice between them, but she was enjoying herself. And even the buzz of her cell phone in her pants pocket for the sixth time—yes, she'd kept count—couldn't ruin it.

Surrender to the demands of her parents to arrive at their home and perform like a perfect show pony?

Or sit here and indulge in this brooding, bearded, sexy enigma with long, dark hair and piercing bright eyes?

Her Harvard education wasn't needed to make this decision.

And in a year where she'd been questioning so many of her choices—her career trajectory, her relationships, hell, the flavor of jelly on her English muffin—tossing out her usual reserve to talk up this fiercely beautiful stranger had been her best decision yet.

Even if initially everything from the stiff set of his massive shoulders to the cold of his stark facial features to the grim line of his carnal mouth had initially told her to fuck off. Although, someone should really inform him that lips that full, that sensual could never truly flatten...

"You're staring."

Mycah hesitated, beer-bottle-number-three a couple of inches away from her mouth. The blush tried to crawl up her throat to her face as she lifted her gaze from his lips to his narrowed blue-gray eyes. And if it hadn't been beer-bottle-number-three, maybe that rush of heat would've met its destination, but a little liquid courage and a lot of I-don't-give-a-damn went a long way toward eroding modesty.

Besides, Achilles hadn't said those two words as other men would've—flirtatiously, with an invitation for her to tell him more about how hot she found him.

No, his words had been a statement of fact, as no-nonsense as his black Henley and scuffed boots. Almost a challenge...an accusation. Why did that have arousal eddying low in her belly?

"I am." Challenge accepted. She sipped from her beer. "Why does that bother you? Because it does. Bother you, that is."

His eyes narrowed even farther. "Because I'm not an animal in a zoo."

She rocked back on the stool, only her fingers clutching the edge of the bar preventing her from losing her balance. Blinking, she gaped at him. Shocked. Stung. Angry.

Slowly twisting around, she signaled for the bartender. When the woman who'd been eye-banging Achilles all night approached, Mycah swirled a finger around his empty shot glass and nearly empty beer mug. "Another round for him, please. On me." His eyebrows jacked down low over his bright gaze, but Mycah shot up a hand, forestalling any argument. "Oh, no, this is about me, not you." Glancing at the woman behind the bar, Mycah flashed her a tight smile. "Please bring those drinks."

"What the hell is that supposed to mean?" Achilles demanded on a low rumble that rippled over her skin, vibrated in her taut nipples and echoed lower, much lower.

That voice of thunder had been wreaking havoc on her all night, and though he'd pissed her off with that unfair comment about treating him like an animal, her body apparently didn't give a damn.

"Hold on." She drank from her beer, waiting until his shot of Jameson and Guinness had been replenished. Only then did she lean forward and meet his gaze, unflinching and all business. "Was she Black?" When he stared back at her, confusion flickering in his eyes, she explained, "The woman I'm the substitute for and getting thrown attitude at on her behalf. Was she Black?"

His scowl could've peeled the paint off the Longfellow Bridge. "What the fuck? Are you actually calling me racist?"

She crossed her legs, cocking her head to the side. "If the bigotry fits…"

"Woman, I know the lighting in this place is for shit, but this skin is brown. My mother was Hawaiian."

Of course, she'd suspected Hawaiian or maybe another Polynesian culture. It was in his high forehead, bold cheekbones, beautiful wide mouth, his thick, dark hair, in his skin kissed by the sun and wind.

And yet, right now, she focused on none of that.

Was.

That *was* shimmered with grief even as *mother* and *Hawaiian* rang with pride. Hurt for him echoed in her chest. For his loss. His pain.

"And your father?"

A shutter fell over his face, and that, too, echoed inside her.

"My father was an asshole."

She nodded. God, did she get that. But that particular trait transcended race, religion, creed and culture.

"You're not a misogynist. Or rather, you don't resent all women. Because when I arrived, you and the bartender—" she dipped her head in the direction of the tattooed brunette on the other end of the bar "—were basically eye-banging each other—in a respectful way.

So there's something about me that's had your back up from the moment I sat down and opened my mouth."

He didn't say anything, but he did knock back the shot of Jameson.

"The tattoos?" Mycah tapped her fingernails on the bar top, swinging from side to side on the stool, scrutinizing that impassive face. "But for all you know, I could have ink underneath this pantsuit..." The truth slammed into her, and she straightened. "That's it, isn't it? The pantsuit. You think I'm slumming it."

He still didn't say anything. Didn't confirm her guess.

But he damn sure didn't deny it, either.

And it hurt. More than it should considering he was a stranger, and she didn't even know his last name.

"You don't know me," she whispered.

"Then tell me why you're here." He propped an arm on the bar and leaned forward until she could detect the ring of lighter blue around his dark irises. Until she could inhale his woodsy pine-and-fresh-rain scent underneath the beer. "And don't lie this time," he ordered in a soft tone that a less discerning person would've called kindness. And that person would be an idiot.

She was tempted to tell him to go fuck himself. That she didn't owe him answers, and he didn't deserve any part of her.

But there was a part of her that wanted—no, *needed*—to prove him wrong. Needed to share something with this man, whom she wouldn't see again, that she couldn't with anyone else. Maybe *because* she wouldn't see him again. He couldn't use the information against her. Couldn't throw it back in her face. Couldn't call her ungrateful or disloyal.

She needed to be…honest. For once in her life, she needed to be honest with someone and with herself.

"Family." The confession slid out of her before she could corral it. "I'm hiding from family."

She could tell him so much more. Like how as soon as her plane had landed at Logan International Airport, her parents had been blowing up her phone, leaving increasingly…vociferous voice mails insisting she join them at their home for their latest dinner party. Or how it didn't matter that she'd just arrived home after an eight-hour flight and a weeklong business trip. There wouldn't be welcoming messages of "welcome home" for her. No "We missed you." Just "Get here because we have an odd number of guests and Janet Holloway is bringing her son who's in wealth management. Be presentable, and for the love of God, don't embarrass us with talk of your boring job."

She could share how since she didn't put it past either one of her parents to send their butler—yes, in this day and age they still had a *butler*—to Mycah's house to hunt her down, she'd escaped to the bar.

But Mycah didn't tell him any of that. She just left it at hiding. Because that alone was incredibly…sad.

And the second after she uttered the word, she fought the pointless urge to snatch the truth back from between them.

Achilles's expression didn't alter; it remained as still, as stony, as it had when he'd basically dared her to prove him wrong. Yet his eyes… His eyes no longer resembled shards of ice. They were heated. And fierce with an emotion that surpassed sympathy.

"Me, too."

She stared at him. Shocked. Two simple words. But like a decoder ring from a cereal box, the words unlocked the meaning of his gaze.

Connection.

Affliction.

Gratification.

"Who would've thought we would find ourselves here?" She surrendered to the desire that had been pulsing within her since spotting him the moment she'd entered the bar. Reaching out, she captured a dense lock of his long hair, rubbed the silken strands between her thumb and forefinger. Her palm itched to scrape over that thick beard. Achilles's sharply indrawn breath echoed between them, but he didn't pull away. Instead, he watched her, those lupine eyes steady and unblinking on her face. On a trembling inhale, she released his hair and leaned back, reaching for her beer and moistening her parched throat. "On common ground," she added, her voice uneven as she attempted a note of levity.

Mimicking her, Achilles lifted his own ale and drank from it. The taut moment vibrated with tension, but then he arched an eyebrow and said, "Yeah, amazing, considering you believe Daniel Craig is a better James Bond than Sean Connery."

She snorted. "I said what I said."

Achilles shook his head. "Blasphemy," he muttered.

Mycah laughed, and when his beautiful mouth quirked again, she mentally chalked in a point for her.

She was a businesswoman, and even if her parents refused to acknowledge it, a damn successful one.

Yet... In this moment, all her accomplishments seemed to fade in comparison with one faint, reluctant smile.

Oh, she was in deep.

And she wanted more of him.

The thought jolted through her before she could cage it. There was no getting rid of it. Not when the idea had already sown deep and even now its roots were spreading, reaching, growing...

Her heart thudded against her rib cage, a heavy bass that reverberated in her sex. In the space of one breath to the next, the arousal that had been frolicking in her veins all evening had flashed into a serious, I'm-not-fucking-around fire.

For the first time in her twenty-nine years, she wanted to jump into the flames and burn.

"You're staring again."

"I am." She switched her legs, recrossing them. And damn his too-observant gaze; he didn't miss the gesture. Probably knew why she did it, too. Not that the action alleviated the sweet pain pulsing inside her. "Does it still bother you?"

"Depends."

"On?"

"Why you're staring."

She slicked the tip of her tongue over her lips, an unfamiliar case of nerves making themselves known. Again, his eyes caught the tell, dropping to her mouth, resting there, and the blast of heat that exploded inside her damn near fused her to the barstool. What he did with one look… Jesus, it wasn't fair.

"Because you're so stareable. Don't do that," she insisted, no, *implored* when he stiffened, his eyes going glacial. Frustration stormed inside her, releasing in a sharp clap of laughter. "This is ridiculous. The ability to communicate is literally in my job description but I seem to fuck it up with you." She huffed out a breath, shaking her head. "You should grant me leeway because you don't know me, and I don't know you. And you—all of you—" she waved her hand up and down "—are a lot."

"A lot of what?" His body didn't loosen; his face remained shuttered. But that voice…

She shivered. Her breath caught. Her breasts swelled. Her thighs squeezed. Was it possible to orgasm from a voice alone? She might be the test case.

"A lot of—" she spread out her arms the length of his shoulders "—mass. A lot of attitude." She exhaled, her hands dropping to her thighs. "A lot of beauty," she murmured with a tremble she hated but couldn't erase. "A lot of pride. A lot of…" Fire. Darkness. Danger. Shelter.

Passion. So much passion. And sex. A promise of hot, burn-her-alive-and-leave-nothing-but-ashes sex.

Her fingers curled into her palm.

"A lot of intensity," she finished.

Achilles stared at her. And she fought not to fidget under his hooded gaze. Struggled to remain still as he leaned forward. That tantalizing, woodsy scent beckoned her closer.

"Mycah, come here."

She should be rebelling; she should be stiffening in offense at that rumbled order. Should be. But no. Instead, a weight she hadn't consciously been aware of tumbled off her shoulders. Allowing her to breathe deeper...freer. Because as Achilles gripped the lapel of her jacket and drew her closer, wrinkling the silk, he also slowly peeled away Mycah Hill, the business executive who carried the responsibilities of several departments... Mycah Hill, the eldest daughter of Laurence and Cherise Hill, who bore the burden of their financial irresponsibility and unrealistic expectations.

In their place stood Mycah, the vulnerable woman who wanted to let go. Who *could* let go. Just this once.

So as he reeled her in, she went willingly, until their faces hovered barely an inch apart. Until their breaths mingled. Until the fire from his bright gaze heated her skin.

This close, she glimpsed the faint smattering of freckles across the tops of his lean cheeks and the high bridge of his nose. The light cinnamon spots should've detracted from the sensual brutality of his features. But they didn't. In an odd way, they enhanced it.

Had her wanting to dot each one with the tip of her tongue.

"What?" she whispered.

"Say it again." He released her jacket and trailed surprisingly gentle fingers up her throat. "I want to find out for myself what the lie tastes like on your mouth."

Lust flashed inside her, hot, searing. Consuming.

God, she liked it.

If she wasn't careful, she could easily come to crave it.

"Do you still think I'm slumming it?" she murmured.

Achilles stared at her. "I don't care."

She blinked, not certain how she felt about that answer. "Why?"

"Because." He didn't remove his gaze from hers as he lifted a hand to her lips, stroked a thumb across the bottom one. "I want be buried inside here." He pressed against her. Hard. "I want to get lost in there." His eyes flicked down to her thighs. Between them. "I want that more than I dislike your…suit."

No man had ever talked to her like that. And his words hurled kindling on the inferno already burning inside her. She wasn't a stranger to men. Even enjoyed them. But never had she felt so desired. No, that didn't describe this. Never had she felt so *vital*. As if she were as necessary to him as food, as water…as oxygen.

She knew what she looked like. Knew what she brought to the table. Also knew her connections, her name, her pedigree were as much an enticement as her face or her body. Sometimes even more so.

Yet this man wanted her in spite of those trappings. Those…albatrosses.

That deepened her hunger for him.

She didn't analyze it. Just accepted it.

More than that. She ached for it.

"So… Am I closing out tabs here or what?"

Mycah jerked straight, her head snapping to the side to meet the narrowed gaze of the bartender. Out of her peripheral vision, she caught Achilles slowly leaning back. Behaving much less "caught in the act." Which was ridiculous on Mycah's part since it hadn't been her who'd been making visual promises to get naked with the bartender.

"Yes," he said to the other woman without the least bit of guilt or regret coating his voice. "You can close out both of them." He reached into his back pocket.

"That's not necessary—"

He shot her a hooded glance. "Oh, it is." Returning his attention to the bartender, he removed several bills that appeared more than enough to cover the tabs and laid them on the bar top. "Close out both and keep the change."

Rising from the stool, he held out his hand toward Mycah, palm up. For a long moment, she stared at that big hand with its long fingers and clean nails. Not only was she about to place her hand in his, but so much more. Her body. Her pleasure. Her safety.

All of that with a man whom she'd known for less than three hours.

It was crazy. Nonsensical. So not her...

She slid her palm over his. Tangled her fingers with his.

And when he tugged her to her feet, she went, her chest brushing his, her thighs nudging his. The heavy weight of his cock branding her belly.

She closed her eyes, lust spiraling through her in a heated glide that incinerated breath and any lingering doubt.

"Let me hear you say it." His other hand gripped her waist, squeezed it. She locked her jaw to contain the whimper that climbed her throat. With a will she hadn't known she possessed, she forced the needy sound back down. "Use that pretty mouth and tell me this is what you want."

"If you expect me to cry foul tomorrow, I won't. No regrets, Achilles." She inhaled a deep breath and tilted her head, studying him. "Now, if you'll let me go, we can get out of here. I can grab a room at whatever hotel you're staying at for whenever we're…finished for the night."

"Finished for the night," he enunciated, a note of incredulity imbedded in his voice. But in the next instant it was replaced by a darker, hungrier tone that vibrated through her, thrumming in her breasts, low in her belly, high in her sex. "What dickless wonders had you in their bed and were satisfied with being *finished for the night*?" He snarled those words with such a healthy dose of scorn that even if she'd suddenly lost her hearing she wouldn't have missed it.

Maybe she should've been embarrassed at his astonishment. But the fact that he seemed insulted on her behalf and angry at the men who'd shortchanged her alleviated some of the sting.

"I think…" She cleared her throat, but the lust thickening her voice didn't evaporate. To hell with it. "I think you should stop talking so we can get out of here and go catch a cab."

He made a sound low in his throat that could've been a laugh or a grunt.

Both had warmth spilling inside her.

Both had her chest squeezing tight.

Both had danger alarms blinking like warning signs on an unlit road.

And allowing him to guide her from the bar, she didn't heed them.

Three

For the first time since arriving at the luxurious five-star hotel with its over-the-top decor, Achilles was thankful for the arrangements his father's estate had made. While he still cringed at the floor-to-ceiling windows that had him itching to yank the drapes closed against the Boston skyline and terrible feeling of exposure, Mycah no doubt appreciated the panoramic view.

What would she think of his cabin? Or the mountains that surrounded it? Would she appreciate the beauty there? Or would the silence, the solitude, the lack of amenities bore her inside a couple of days?

He mentally shook his head. Why was he even entertaining those questions? They were pointless because this—Mycah in his hotel room, the sex that would happen—wouldn't go past tonight.

But they did have tonight.

And from the moment she'd stood up from that stool, confirming every fantasy about her body, he'd been exceedingly grateful to deities both Christian and pagan for tonight.

As she glided across the sunken living area into the dining room, the lights from the crystal chandelier hitting her tight, raw-honey curls, his hungry gaze dropped to the sensual sway of her round hips. To the tight perfection of her full ass. The thickness of her thighs. And when she peeled off her suit jacket, laying it over the back of a dining room chair, his fascinated stare rose to the pull of material across her breasts. His fingers curled, straightened. He didn't even have to close his eyes to imagine the feel of her undoubtedly firm yet tender flesh.

Unbidden, like an animal scenting its mate—there he went again with the fanciful shit—he followed her. But not to touch her, even though the need to do so rode him hard. Like a child with sticky fingers and his face pressed against a candy store window, he enjoyed looking at her. Because no matter how much he wished it didn't, her beauty captivated him. Dark brown, heavily lashed eyes that seemed full of secrets yet brimming with a vulnerable truth. Arrogant cheekbones, a patrician nose, stubborn but delicate jaw and chin, and a carnal mouth that he couldn't stop staring at. Couldn't stop picturing working him over until he trembled and begged...

"Do you want me to get rid of my clothes so they don't remind you of who I am? Would that make this easier for you?" she asked, turning away from the wall of glass, her fingers fiddling with the top button of her nearly sheer shirt.

A teasing note infiltrated her voice, but he caught the hint of stiffness beneath. The...insecurity. And he'd put it there with his words, his personal hang-ups. It was his responsibility to erase that doubt. It didn't belong between them. Not here. Not tonight.

"Is that what you think?" He edged closer, cocked his head. Pinching a curl, he tugged it and watched as heat flared bright in those chocolate eyes and her carnal lips parted on a soft gasp. "That you can just strip off that suit, slip out of those shoes and I won't be reminded of, what? How soft and delicate this skin is?" He rubbed the back of his finger down the satin of her cheek. "Of how cultured and sexy this voice is?"

He lowered his hand to her throat, necklacing the slim column. If she'd stiffened or shoved at him— protested the hold in any way—he would've released her. But she didn't. No, Mycah's lashes fluttered, and she slightly leaned into his palm, as if relishing the show of dominance. His cock jerked behind his zipper, blood roaring south to fill his flesh in a flood that left him almost light-headed. He ground his teeth against the lust that scalded him.

Inhaling, he dipped his head, dragged his nose up the tendon that ran along the side of her neck. "What? You think taking off your clothes will somehow erase this scent that's grace, woman...sex?" He shook his head, brushing his lips over the line of her jaw and nearly growling at the skin-to-skin contact. "No, Mycah. Stripping can't make me forget who you are. And it for damn sure wouldn't make things easier for me. Just. Fucking. Harder."

"Achilles."

"Yeah?" He grazed another caress over her jaw, her chin, unable to help himself. Not sure he wanted to.

"Kiss me. Please."

So demanding.

So polite.

And both had him crushing his mouth to hers in a greedy onslaught.

That first taste. It crashed into him like a meteor set on a collision course with Earth. Hot. Cataclysmic. Fatalistic.

She opened for him without hesitation, and he dived deep, taking immediate advantage. The kiss was… carnage. It left him wrecked, wide open and damn near shaking. He sent mental orders to his hands to be gentle on her hair, to not fist the strands so tight, to not pull so hard. But they didn't listen. They didn't loosen. Thank God Mycah didn't seem to mind. No, the opposite. From the hot, tiny whimpers that he swallowed directly from her greedy tongue, she appeared to want it…crave more of it.

So he gave it to her.

He tugged on those rough silk curls, hauling her head back, angling it and diving deeper. Consuming more. Leaving nothing untouched, undiscovered. Every lick, every suck, every lap stoked a need that crackled and raged. But he wasn't satisfied with burning in those flames. He wanted to be devoured by them.

Untangling one hand from her hair, he lowered it to her throat again, feeling the mad thrum of her pulse under his palm. Reveling in the rush of it. Because it was for him. He sent blood pumping through her, excitement and lust rushing through her. *Him.*

The knowledge lit up his veins, and he snatched his mouth from hers, ignoring her small cry of disappointment to latch on to that thin patch of skin. He tongued it, tasting the richness of her scent, grunting at the bite of her nails in his shoulders. His hips punched forward at that hint of pain, mating with the pleasure twisting and bucking inside him. He ground his cock against the soft swell of her belly, growling like an animal. His gut clenched, lust a vise clamping tighter. And tighter.

"Fuck," he muttered against her damp skin.

Lifting his head, he captured her mouth once more, unable not to. He *needed*… God, he hated saying that word even in his head. Hated that it was true. But he did. He ached for her taste on his lips. Hurt for the cushion of her flesh against his throbbing dick. Hungered for the almost plaintive sounds that escaped her—that let him know he wasn't in this struggle by himself.

Though it cost him, he levered back and away from her. But just for a moment. Long enough to reach behind him, grab a fistful of his shirt and pull it over his head. Lips swollen and eyes hooded, Mycah watched him. And as he dropped the bunched cotton to the floor, she lifted her hands to the top of her own shirt, but he stopped her with a hard shake of his head.

"Let me." With fingers that suddenly felt too big, too

clumsy, he plucked at the little pearl buttons, pushing them through the corresponding holes.

His heart kicked against his rib cage in steel-toe boots as he revealed smooth brown flesh encased in light purple lace. All moisture fled his mouth, and he didn't stop until he skated his palms over her shoulders, sliding her shirt down her arms and to the floor.

"Fucking beautiful." The last word scratched against his vocal cords as he traced a path along the pretty edge where lace met skin.

Gooseflesh broke out where his fingertip tread, and he jerked his gaze up to her face, amazement sparking inside his chest. Yes, she'd allowed him to strip her of her shirt, let him touch these gorgeous breasts, but still... Part of him still couldn't believe it. Still wondered when she'd change her mind.

"Whatever you do tonight," she said, grasping his larger hand in her smaller, more delicate one and pressing it harder to her flesh, "don't treat me like I'll break. I can take it, take you. Give me all of you, Achilles. Don't hold back on me."

"You don't know what you're asking, Mycah, telling a man like me not to hold back."

As...ominous as that sounded, he'd gone into that bar to forget about his dead sperm donor, about brothers he hadn't known existed, about being forced into a world he wanted nothing to do with.

About being rejected, scorned by that world—again.

So yeah, he'd gone there seeking nothing more than to lose himself in oblivion—alcohol and sex. And that didn't lend itself toward control or setting limitations on himself. And once he got his mouth on that dusky valley between her breasts or that dip where her torso and thigh connected—or her dark, wet sex… Yeah, control would be a pipe dream.

Mycah shifted closer and lifted her arms, burrowing her hands into his hair, her nails scraping over his scalp.

"Do your worst."

He shuddered, at her words and at her touch. Pleasure streaked through him. Groaning, he gripped her hips and, hiking her in the air, nudged the chairs out of the way and set her on top of the dining room table. Her soft, startled gasp segued into a sharp cry as he bent over her and sucked a diamond-hard, lace-covered nipple between his lips.

His own low moan almost drowned her out, his mouth insistent, impatient. Ravenous. He pulled on the beaded tip, drawing on her. The pinpricks dancing across his scalp from her restless fingers only stirred him, encouraged him. With his free hand, he unsnapped the front clasp of her bra and quickly removed it, cursing as he cupped her flesh.

"Achilles," she whispered, twisting against him, thrusting her breasts into his mouth. "Please."

There was no way he could deny such a pretty plea. Switching to the other mound, he nuzzled the neglected nipple, then plied it with licks and sensual laps. By the time he finished, skimming his lips down her damp torso, her chest heaved, her stomach going concave under his tongue. But he didn't pause, couldn't. Not when passion and need swept him up in an undertow so fierce, he was powerless against it. Not when lust clawed and howled inside him like a voracious beast that demanded to be satisfied.

Not when he doubted he could ever be satisfied.

Even as the sacrilegious thought skipped through his head and his heart thudded in protest, he pressed a hand to her chest, gently urging her to lie back on the table. She watched him, a wary expression flashing across her face.

"Trust me?" Why he asked that, he didn't know. He didn't need her trust; that's not what tonight was about. But he didn't try to retract the question. Partly because, though it didn't make sense, he wanted it. He wanted her assent.

After a moment, she slowly dipped her head, sending relief coursing through him. "In this—" her gaze flicked down her bare torso to where his fingers lightly gripped the tab at her waist "—yes. I trust you."

It was enough.

In quick work, he freed her of the pants, taking her panties with them, pausing only to remove the heels from her slender feet. Placing fleeting kisses along her instep, he trailed a worshipful path back up her inner thighs. He closed his eyes, inhaling her earthy musk, savoring it. Craving it on his tongue.

"Achilles." Mycah cupped his head, her beautiful legs tightening around him. Preventing him from moving. "I haven't… I've never… I don't— Hell."

He stopped, settling into one of the dining room chairs as if having a woman spread out before him like a delicious buffet was a common occurrence. No, not a woman. Mycah. And there was nothing common about her. Trying not to stare at her trembling breasts with their beaded, dark nipples or the lush beauty of her thighs or the soaked, swollen folds of her sex was a struggle that defied human strength and veered into something out of mythological trials.

"You haven't what, Mycah? Had a man's mouth on you? Do you want me stop?" Jesus Christ, it might kill him—especially when he could *see* the evidence of how much she wanted him on her flesh—but he would. Cold anger pulsed inside him for the selfish pricks who hadn't given her this.

"No, of course I've…had a man's mouth on me. I can't believe I'm having this conversation with you while you're literally sitting between my legs," she muttered, pressing the heel of her palm over her eyes. She propped herself up on her elbows, curls wild around her face and shoulders, her face an adorable mixture of confusion and surprise.

"Do you want me to stop?" he asked again. Because to him—and his dick—that was the most important issue here.

"No," she whispered, her eyes glazing over.

"Then what have you never done, Mycah?"

"This." She waved a hand down her body, encompassing him. "On a table. With the lights so…bright," she finished, her voice containing a tinge of embarrassment. "Could we possibly go to the, I don't know, couch or bed, where I don't feel so…exposed? I mean, people eat on this table."

"No."

She stared at him. Blinked. "No?"

"No." He shifted to the edge of the chair, simultaneously gripping her hips and tugging her closer to the end of the table. "You told me not to treat you like you're fragile, like you'll break. Light won't break you. Pushing you out of a comfort zone won't break you." He pushed his face into the fragrant space where her torso and thigh met. Inhaled. Growled. "Like you said, people eat on this table. Well, so will I."

He dived into her.

Palming her thighs, he spread her wide and feasted on her. He dragged his tongue through her folds, losing himself in the sweet, spiced taste of her. Taking his time to lick and nibble. To explore and discover what made her legs tremble, that little bud of flesh flinch. What drew whimper after whimper. He became a connoisseur in everything Mycah.

Though his dick ached, he could stay here, his mouth buried against her, pleasuring her. An inane thought crept in his mind, there and gone before he could banish it: purpose. *I've found my purpose. Giving this woman ecstasy.*

"Achilles." Once more her fingers had found their way to his hair, tangling and pulling, holding him close. Her hips bucked, rocked, demanded. There existed no ambiguity about what she needed from him. "Please. I need…" A sound between a whimper and a cry escaped her but the abrupt flex of her ass telegraphed her request. "Please," she whispered.

Before, he'd thought her pleas pretty. This time, they shredded him. And that primal part of him that desired—hell, was *obligated*—to provide what she asked of him. Sucking the bundle of nerves that crested her sex, he thrust two fingers inside her. Deep. Hard.

She screamed.

She clamped down on him and, between his mouth and fingers, he gave her every measure of the orgasm, not stopping until she fell limp on the table. Her pants lanced the quiet of the room, and his harsh breaths underscored hers.

Fuck. Lust strung him tight, and if he didn't get inside her, he was going to snap.

He shot to his feet, the chair beneath him falling backward. With his body moving before his mind could fully deliver the order, he scooped Mycah up in his arms, cradling her. He calculated the distance to the bedroom, but his cock determined the couch was closer, and he headed there. Mycah didn't open her eyes as he gently deposited her on the sofa that was easily double the size of his at home. But he didn't remove his gaze from her while he quickly stripped his remaining clothes and boots, pausing only long enough to remove a condom from his wallet.

"Hey." He knelt beside the couch, cupping her face and tilting it, sweeping his thumb over her cheekbone. "Look at me."

Her lashes fluttered, then lifted. Satisfaction punched him in the chest when her pleasure-glazed brown eyes met his. Because he'd put that look there. The feeling was primitive. It was arrogant. But fuck if he didn't own it.

"You good? You still with me?"

She blinked, the haze clearing. Her gaze roamed over

his face then lower, down his shoulders, chest and lower still, taking in his dick that stood at rock-hard attention. He didn't try to hide from her, fisting his erection, stroking it. Letting her see just what she did to him.

"Yes, I'm still with you." She reached for him, covering his hand with hers. Replacing his hands with hers.

A full-body shiver racked him as her delicate fingers wrapped around him, squeezed him. His head bowed, palms flattened on his thighs. And he watched her— watched her touch him. Undo him.

"Enough, baby," he ground out, gently sweeping aside her devastating fists. "I want to finish inside of you."

Picking up the protection, he ripped it open, swiftly sheathed himself and then climbed onto the couch. He crouched over her, one knee separating her thighs, the other planted on the floor. The head of his dick kissed the wet, tiny opening of her sex, and he shook from that barely there caress, yet he paused.

As much as it cost him, he gripped the arm of the couch and pressed his forehead to hers, carefully crushed his mouth to hers...and breathed Mycah in. As he parted his lips, slowly slid his tongue into her, he mimicked the action with his cock.

Thrust.

Penetrated.

Buried deep.

Heat. A liquid heat that scalded and had him drowning at the same time.

He clenched his jaw, his fingers curling around the couch's arm so tight they pulsed in protest. His muscles howled with the need to move, but the stranglehold she had on his dick… Too tight. Almost painfully tight. And too fucking perfect. He didn't want to break it.

Tearing his mouth from hers, he scattered hard kisses to the corners of her mouth, chin, cheekbones, temples, forehead.

"Talk to me, Mycah." He studied her, searching her face for any sign of discomfort. Her sex fluttered around his dick, as if acclimating to his width, his length. And he granted her that time. Still, before he did anything else, he wanted those words to move. "You okay? Tell me what you need from me."

Her tongue wet her full lips, and she met his gaze. "Don't hold back with me."

Groaning, he hooked a hand underneath her leg, and withdrawing until only the tip of him remained notched inside her, he thrust home. Their twin groans saturated the room, snapping his control. Her nails bit into his waist, and that added a flare of pain to the sensory overload that catapulted him into this erotic storm.

He didn't fight it. Didn't want to. No, he willingly became a part of it. He let go, sweeping Mycah up with him, riding her, fucking her with an abandon that should've alarmed him. And if he'd cared enough to slow down, to analyze why this woman affected him in a way no other did, he might've been scared. But he didn't slow. Didn't analyze. Didn't care.

Flipping them over together, he buried his hands in her curls, dragging her head down and fusing their mouths together as he slammed up inside her, urging her to take him even as he did the taking. And she obeyed that unspoken command. Her hips crashed into his over and over, she rose and lowered, doing a lewd dance that threatened to send them into the sweetest, dirtiest oblivion.

Mycah trembled, her sex quivering around him, and heeding that signal of a looming release, Achilles reached between them and circled that slick, swollen button between her feminine folds. Circled, rubbed. Pinched.

With a high, hoarse scream, she came.

And a couple of strokes later, he went with her.

Even as he hurled over that edge, he knew one truth...

Once wouldn't be enough.

Four

The elevator doors opened with a quiet hiss and Achilles stepped onto the executive floor of Farrell International. It'd been three months since he'd attended the reading of his *father's* will. He barely managed to suppress a shudder. God, even thinking that word still had a fist of disgust and anger lodged in the base of his throat. It'd been three months since he'd arrived in Boston to find out about Barron's death. Since he'd gained two half brothers. Since he'd become a billionaire who owned and ran one-third of an international conglomerate.

But in those ninety-and-some-change days, he'd yet to stop feeling like an impostor. Yet to stop feeling like the fifty-first part of a fifty-piece puzzle that the manufacturer mistakenly added to the box.

The Feral Farrell.

That's what they called him.

Not to Achilles's face. No, Boston's so-called polite society and his older brother Cain's many business associates weren't brave enough to risk their reputation or bottom line to do something as stupid as blatantly insult a Farrell. Bastard or not.

More specifically, insult Cain, the rightful heir, the son Barron Farrell kept and acknowledged. They really couldn't care less about offending a man they didn't believe would be around a year from now.

They weren't wrong.

Sliding his hands into the front pockets of his suit pants, Achilles kept his gaze focused straight ahead, not glancing around and taking in the quiet but obvious wealth of the executive floor. It wasn't the first or the fifteenth time he'd been here. But the art on the walls that cost more than his entire cabin or the furniture that had most likely been handpicked by some interior designer who catered to celebrities and presidents alike unnerved him *every time* he stepped foot up here. Hell, even the smell would make a great candle labeled "Money to Burn."

Achilles silently growled, battling the urge to yank the tie from his hair, rip this restricting suit jacket from his shoulders and flip one of these desks like an enraged reality housewife. That would give these people a show. That's why they watched him like a hawk, after all. Waiting for him to lose his shit like an uncivilized sideshow act. Just so they could say, *I told you so. He's not like his brothers. Not like Cain, the heir. Or Kenan, the charmer. He's not one of us.*

Again… They wouldn't be wrong.

He wasn't Cain, who, unlike Achilles and Kenan, Barron Farrell had kept instead of abandoned, and trained from day one to run his international company. Achilles wasn't Kenan Rhodes, who, though he was another illegitimate son, had been adopted and raised by an influential and powerful Boston family.

No, Achilles was the ex-con, semireclusive bastard who preferred the company of code and computers to people.

There'd been only one time since he'd arrived in this city that he'd felt wanted…needed. As it often did, more than he cared to admit, his mind flickered with images of that sex-soaked night in a five-star hotel with a beautiful woman he was half-convinced he'd conjured up. Only the scratches he'd carried on his shoulders and on his waist and the chafing on his dick the next morning had proved to him that he hadn't. Those and the dreams that continued to haunt him like erotic wraiths all these months later.

How many times had he woken up, shaking with lust, back bowed, lips twisted in a snarl? How many times had he found himself searching the crowded streets for that familiar, stunning face? Or cocking his head, listening for a certain low, sultry voice?

One night. That had been the limit he'd set. And he didn't regret it. Because as his unconscious mind revealed, Mycah could've become an obsession with him. And he didn't need anything—not obligations, not promises, not brothers, not obsessions—holding him here when his year came due.

Nothing would hold him back. He would be free to return home, unfettered.

Fuck.

He deliberately inhaled a breath, quieted the riot of morose thoughts swirling in his head.

None of this mattered. None of it changed the fact that he'd promised to remain in Boston for a year to helm Farrell International with half brothers he hadn't known existed three months ago.

He'd made his billion-dollar bed and now he had to lie in it.

"Good morning, Mr. Farrell." Charlene Gregg, Cain's executive assistant, greeted him with a warm but professional smile as he approached her desk. "They're waiting for you in the conference room."

Achilles nodded and strode past her. Why Cain insisted on including him in these business meetings eluded him. Contract negotiations, board or acquisitions meetings… Having Kenan there since he was a marketing genius made sense. But Achilles? He couldn't give a damn about any of it. Just leave him to ride out the next nine months on the IT's eighth floor, where he'd carved out a place for himself, and he would be fine.

Clenching his jaw, he grasped the handle to the conference room door and pressed it down.

"…reputation precedes you— Here he is." Cain stood from one of the black leather corporate chairs that flanked the long wood table, Kenan rising, as well.

"We were waiting on you to arrive before we started the interview, Achilles."

Achilles dipped his head in acknowledgment, quietly shutting the door behind him.

"Sorry. I had a call and was held up," he said.

Partly true. He'd been on the phone with one of the sales reps about possible new virus protection software, but it'd ended nearly a half hour earlier. It's what he'd started working on after the call that had consumed his attention and made him lose track of time. But he couldn't share that with Cain and Kenan. Not with anyone.

He moved toward the chair next to Kenan and avoided his younger brother's too-sharp gaze. God, for someone who constantly seemed to wear a smile the man was too fucking perceptive. It annoyed the hell out of him.

As if reading Achilles's mind, Kenan smiled wider, a gleam in his eyes. "No problem. We know how much you insist on attending these meetings, so we didn't want to go forward without you."

Thank God he'd been an only child for thirty years.

"Achilles, we were just starting," Cain said. The corner of his mouth twitched as if he were attempting to imprison a smile at Kenan's not-so-subtle smart-ass dig. Three months ago, Cain Farrell would've seared the paint off the walls with a scowl at Kenan's antics. But now, he fought back a grin. Funny what falling in love and getting engaged did to a man. Cain turned toward the woman rising from the seat across the table, sweeping an arm in her direction. "Let me introduce you to Mycah Hill. She's interviewing for the VP of operations position."

Mycah.

Shock, icy and rough, slammed into him. Every muscle in his body locked as he stared at the woman across from him. The woman who had let him lose himself in her body on several surfaces of a hotel room. The woman who, months later, refused to be evicted from his head.

Goddamn, she was…gorgeous.

As if Fate were having a slow day and decided to play a game of "Whom Can I Fuck with Now?" Mycah could've been plucked right from his memories and set down in this conference room. The same tight, honey-brown spirals that even now he could feel over his palm. The same beautiful face with its oval-shaped, dark brown eyes, sculpted cheekbones, lush, decadent mouth and delicate but stubborn chin. The same thick, curvaceous body that conveyed a sensual strength that had his chest squeezing and his dick hardening.

What the hell was she—what had Cain said her full name was? Mycah Hill?—doing here? No, wait. A job. The position of vice president of operations. At the company Achilles owned a third of. His company. What were the odds she hadn't known?

Even if she hadn't been aware of his identity that night in the bar—and he believed she hadn't since the news about him and Kenan hadn't broken yet—she damn well did now. The media scrutiny on the sudden appearance of the two Farrell bastards had been hell since the funeral. And from the moment they met,

Mycah had struck Achilles as a smart woman. And she wouldn't apply for a job without first thoroughly researching the company and its owners.

Yes, she would've walked into this building fore-warned and armed with the information that she would be sitting across from the person she'd seen biblically naked.

That made one of them.

He narrowed his gaze on her, meeting those level espresso eyes. To her credit, she didn't avoid him. Ad-miration and anger tangled in his chest.

What was her plan now? Admit that she knew him? That she'd spent a night under him, over him, spread wide for him?

Or pretend that she'd never laid eyes on him before?

"Mycah, this is Achilles Farrell, our third brother, and Chief Digital Officer of our IT department," Cain continued with the introduction.

Mycah nodded, offering Achilles a polite smile. "It's a pleasure to meet you, Mr. Farrell."

So it was to be option B.

The well-mannered thing to do would've been to reply, but at the moment that was beyond him. He was too busy strong-arming the disappointment and anger barreling through him like a rampaging bull.

Which didn't make any sense.

This disappointment in her. This rage. He'd been more than aware whom he was taking to bed. Known that her pretty talk aside, that if he'd met her on the cobblestone streets of Beacon Hill in the light of day, she wouldn't have anything to do with his rough talk, rough hands and rougher demeanor. Her kind with their flawless pedigree, upper tax bracket, superior education and untouchable society.

Although, he'd proved just how...touchable she was, hadn't he? No matter how much she probably wanted to forget.

Too fucking bad.

Still, he dipped his head, rolling one of the executive chairs back and lowering into it. Kenan shot him an exasperated glance and Achilles returned it with an arched eyebrow.

"Since calling all of us Mr. Farrell could become a little confusing," Cain said, reclaiming his seat, as well, "why don't we go with Cain, Kenan and Achilles?"

Another smile from her, and Achilles curled his fingers into his thigh under the table, remembering how those lips had curled against his own. Had parted so easily and greedily under his own. *Shit.* He shifted his gaze from her to the wall of windows over her shoulder. This interview had to end before he did something monumentally stupid.

Like beg her to give him one more taste of that heady lavender-and-cedar scent...

"I can do that," she agreed.

"Great. Let's get started." Cain passed Achilles a folder, and with no choice he opened it, finding her résumé inside. "We've gone over your résumé, and I'm very familiar with your reputation, which is impeccable. Over at Ryland & Co., you were key in restructuring their policies and departments. Thanks to the programs and streamlined procedures you implemented, the company substantially created higher ROI as well as optimization of workflow. I have to admit, I spoke with certain management personnel over there, and they spoke highly of you and admitted that you helped attain growth and profit for the business. That's a glowing recommendation, but one I already knew. The question is—" Cain rested his forearms and clasped hands on the table "—why are you looking to leave Ryland to come here?"

Mycah didn't immediately answer, instead mimicking Cain's position and meeting his steady gaze, before making visual contact with each of them. Though his eye contact was shorter. Still, Achilles found himself leaning forward, impatient to hear her reply. This woman—professional, reserved, confident—he'd glimpsed that night in the dive bar. But damn if he wasn't reluctantly fascinated by this facet of her.

"Ryland is a good, stable company. I wouldn't have stayed with them for seven years, the last three in the position of VP of operations, if they weren't. But Farrell International isn't just good—it's the best. And here, *I* can be the best. I can start at vice president of operations, but that's just the beginning and not the end of where I can go. I've done all I can at Ryland, and one thing I can't abide is stagnancy. And—" she arched an eyebrow high, the corner of her mouth twitching "—there is the matter of the salary you're offering, which is almost double what I'm making now."

Kenan chuckled. "Honesty. I like it."

Cain cocked his head. "So you wouldn't be satisfied with the position of vice president of operations?"

Again, Mycah copied him. "Would you?" she retorted smoothly.

Cain slowly smiled. "No."

Ambitious. Probably ruthless. Achilles silently snorted. Why wasn't he surprised? Virtues both his half brothers would admire. Achilles had seen those same qualities in the inmates who'd come into the jail and desired to rule the pod, make life fucking miserable for the rest of them who just wanted to get through their sentence with their heads down and as little trouble as possible.

He didn't trust ambition. Didn't trust those who hungered for it and what it brought.

The rest of the interview progressed with no input from him and more questions from Cain and Kenan about her work experience, what she could bring to Farrell International, what she would implement, how she would handle certain business situations. Achilles sat back, wishing he could tune them out. Trying to ignore her presence.

But that was an impossibility.

Her voice vibrated inside him like a tuning fork. Her scent might as well have infiltrated the central air system because it seemed to circulate in the conference room, saturating the air. Why his brothers couldn't sense it confounded him.

He'd tried not looking at her, but... That hair. Those eyes. That mouth. Even her damn throat. There wasn't a damn part of her he could tear his gaze from. Wasn't a part of her he could stare at and not...remember. Not relive.

By the time Cain started to wrap up the interview, Achilles pretended not to notice Kenan's curious side-long glances at his bouncing leg or the vise grip he had on the chair's arms.

The walls weren't closing in on him; he would've recognized the signs of a panic attack. After his release from jail, he'd suffered them often enough. Being locked in a six-by-eight-foot cell for hours on end could do that to a person. But this wasn't that.

No, what pressed in on him now was the weight of her indifference. What twisted his stomach and squeezed his rib cage was the loathing for himself because he fucking cared.

He needed out of here.

Shoving his chair back, he shot to his feet.

Cain frowned, concern darkening his blue-gray eyes. "Achilles, you—"

"I forgot about a phone call I'm expecting," he said by way of explanation for his erratic behavior. "It was nice meeting you, Ms. Hill."

He shoved the words out, and they emerged sounding scraped and rough. Nothing he could do about it. Just as he couldn't do anything about the bemused looks Cain and Kenan threw him. No doubt they were wondering if there was any truth to that Feral Farrell bullshit.

Especially Cain.

They were all in a better place than they had been when Kenan and Achilles first entered Cain's life, but Achilles didn't fool himself. A man as brilliant and as guarded as his older brother didn't allow wolves at his door without first having them at least collared. Cain would've had a background search done on Achilles. His brother had to know about his criminal background. About *why* he'd been locked up.

Unable to meet their gazes any longer—and definitely unable to look at the woman whose very presence drove him away—he strode out of the conference room.

No, that was a lie.

He fled.

Five

Mycah stared down at her new badge, her solemn image gazing back up at her. It belied the nerves buzzing inside her like a swarm of bees.

A day.

Only twenty-four hours after the interview with the three Farrell brothers, and Cain had called, offering her the position of VP of operations. Even though she clutched the badge that granted her access to the office building and executive floor, even though the company handbook and employee contract claimed space in her briefcase, part of her still couldn't believe she was now an employee of one of the most powerful, influential and wealthiest conglomerates in the world.

Her predominant emotion should have been joy or excitement.

Or definitely satisfaction.

A twenty-nine-year-old Black woman in a field dominated by older white men, and she was already making her mark? And this was just the beginning, as she'd told Cain Farrell. So yes, satisfaction should definitely be coursing through her.

But no. The main feeling that she had to lock her knees against, lest she crumble to the elevator floor in an undignified heap?

Relief.

Because as soon as she'd received that call, she could breathe again.

In the interview, Cain had asked about her reasons for wanting to work with Farrell International. She'd been truthful. But not fully.

After all, how could she explain to a prospective employer that she needed this job so that the huge stone wheel slowly grinding her rib cage to dust could finally, *finally* lift? And the name of that stone wheel?

Family.

Right. That wouldn't have gone over well. They would've all stared at her as if she'd suddenly sprouted six fire-breathing heads, then politely ushered her to the conference room door.

Well, maybe one of them wouldn't have. Maybe one of them would've understood.

She briefly closed her eyes, and an image of Achilles Farrell instantly appeared. Not that it required much to summon him to her mind. Physically, they might've indulged in a one-night stand, but mentally? Mentally, she'd conducted a three-month-long affair where he invaded her bed most nights, not leaving her dreams until he'd left her aching and wet—and empty. So damn empty.

Huffing out a breath, she shook her head, staring at the lit elevator button for the eighth floor. As it dimmed, the doors hissed open. Her heart thudded against her sternum, stomach twisting as she stepped out onto the deserted floor. She'd waited until after seven to access the building, checking with security downstairs to make sure the person she needed to see hadn't yet left for the day.

Preparing herself for coming face-to-face with Achilles for the interview had been difficult. And she'd still barely pulled it off. God, the power, the vitality the man emanated... It was a force that slipped under her dress to hum over her skin, skim over her nipples, dance over her belly, slip between her legs... She'd nearly rocked under it, betraying herself to Cain and Kenan Farrell.

Whether in jeans and boots or a perfectly tailored suit, Achilles was potent.

And when his lupine eyes had locked with hers?

She'd lost all thought. Well, not *all*.

Memories of how he'd laid her out on that dining room table to make a feast of her had bombarded her. Of how he'd carried her so tenderly to the couch before taking her so fiercely.

Of how he'd followed through on his promise of not being finished with her for the night.

She hadn't stumbled into her own hotel room until early the next morning, deliciously sore and tired.

And yet somehow, she'd met Achilles's gaze in that

conference room and not revealed that she shook with those memories.

If her mother had been there, she would've beamed with pride over her daughter's ability to lie.

A dull pounding took up above her right eye, a sure sign of a pending migraine. The sooner she got this task over with, the better. She started her position at Farrell International in a week. This wasn't a conversation she could avoid.

The thick carpet silenced the footfalls of her heels as she approached the closed office door. The open blinds on the windows offered her an unfettered view of the long-haired, wolf-eyed giant frowning at the bank of computers on his desk. She stuttered to a halt, her breath catching in her throat. He was so, so... So damn *too*.

Too gorgeous.

Too virile.

Too sexy.

Too wild.

He was the eye of the hurricane, a false calm. One shift, one step either way, and he would devastate you with all that he was.

And God. She closed her eyes, pinched the bridge of her nose. She needed to lay off the late-night Netflix binges.

She lifted her lashes and a bright gaze immediately ensnared hers.

Lowering her arm, she deliberately exhaled.

Hell.

Fixing a smile to her face that felt brittle and fake, she forced her feet forward and opened the closed office door. He rose from his chair, as if the good manners of standing for a woman were reflexive rather than voluntary. The scowl creasing his forehead remained.

"Achilles." Wonder whispered through her that her voice didn't tremble. Because, damn, that glare could burn hydrogen off the sun.

"Kenan told me you were hired. Congratulations." The flat tone carried no sarcasm, no venom, no…nothing. And that bothered her. More than she wanted to admit.

"Thank you." She hesitated, studied him. "You didn't…?"

"Have anything to do with the decision?" he finished her question, then shook his head. "No. I told them whatever they decided was fine with me."

Once more, relief rushed through her, and she glanced away from him. The last of her uncertainty that she hadn't earned this job on her own merit faded away.

"Is that why you're here?" He circled the desk and leaned back against it, crossing his arms over his wide shoulders. She pretended not to notice how the sleeves of his plain white dress shirt strained against his powerful arms. Pretended not to notice the corresponding pull low in her belly. "To make sure I didn't influence the outcome?" He cocked his head. "Or to make sure I did?"

Hurt, dagger sharp and bright, pierced her chest, and she blinked against it. "Is that what you really think? That I wanted you to use our past…association to give me this job?"

"Why are you here?"

Another flash of pain. But this time, she buried it beneath a sheet of ice. She'd learned the coping mechanism early; with parents like hers, she'd acquired defensive skills that would impress a five-star general. If she survived Laurence and Cherise Hill, she damn well could endure this conversation with Achilles Farrell.

"To clear the air. If we're going to be working together—if I'm going to be a vice president for your company—we need to be on the same page. Especially about where we stand as far as being employer and employee."

"Make it plain, Mycah. You're not going to be fucking the boss, and you don't want anyone to know that you have in the past. Is that what you're saying?"

How was it possible to go up in flames that were equal parts embarrassment and lust? It seemed like he twisted everything she said to him. But God, just hearing him growl the word *fuck* and recalling his saying it to her at another time under very different circumstances...

She shook her head. "Look, Achilles, can we start over? It seems like I keep offending you—"

"Why did you pretend not to know me yesterday?" He pushed off the desk, straightening, but he didn't come near her.

Shame flickered through her, and she forced herself to meet his gaze. She'd like to say that she was an honest person, and at her core, she believed she was. God, she had to cling to that belief. But in her family, lies had their many uses. For her parents, lies were tools, a stock in trade. For Mycah and her sister, they were a necessity for survival.

And that's what yesterday had been.

Survival.

"I'm sorry that I misled your brothers—"

"You lied."

"I lied," she murmured. Exhaling a soft breath, she spread her hands out, palms up. "And I'm sorry for the position it put you in. I really am, Achilles." She shifted closer to him, but the ice in his eyes warned her not to come nearer. A shiver worked its way through her. With effort, she forced her hands to her sides instead of rubbing them up and down her arms to ward off the chill. "I'm not asking you to understand or accept my reason, but I'm a woman in a male-dominated business. Even with all my education, the successes that I can recite alphabetically and chronologically, if anyone discovered that I'd had sex with an employer or supervisor, none of what I accomplished would matter. I would be seen only as the woman who made it to the top on her back."

Achilles didn't reply, but he jerked his chin at her, and she took that as the universal man sign to continue. Sighing, she ran a hand through her curls.

"I don't know if your brothers would've fallen into that misogynistic category, but I also know I couldn't chance it."

Because she needed this job.

Not just because she desired to bust through a glass ceiling.

Not just because of the prestige of being an officer with a company that consistently appeared on the Fortune 100.

No, she desperately needed this job because of family. Specifically, her parents.

While the Hill name might belong to old wealth and an older lineage, thanks to Laurence and Cherise's over-indulgent lifestyle, the quarterly business profits of their family company couldn't support them. And so, her parents had come to depend on Mycah's employment—or rather her salary—even as they derided her for that dependence. They considered her job common; it shamed them. Yet they expected her to foot the bill when their allowance ran out. What was an overdue mortgage or car payment or the household staff's salaries going unpaid when the living room had to be redesigned with what was au courant? Why should they concern themselves with inconsequential bills when they had her to cover them?

If it were just them, she might say to hell with it. But it wasn't just them. There was Angelique. Her brilliant fifteen-year-old sister had started high school this year. And not just any high school. A prestigious private academy whose academics rivaled Harvard—and so did the price tag. But she deserved every advantage. And for Angel, Mycah would willingly pay...

Even if it meant continuing to foot the tab for their parents, too.

The throb above Mycah's right eye intensified, and she caged the impulse to rub it. At one time, she'd willingly stripped naked in front of Achilles, had been as vulnerable as a woman could be with a man. But that was then, not now. She couldn't afford to be weak, exposed. This man, so unlike the one who'd taken her mouth even as he'd tenderly and passionately taken her body, offered her no quarter with his merciless stare. He sought a flaw to exploit.

"Was lying the only length you were willing to go to?" He moved forward, closing the distance between them.

He stopped just short of looming over her, but still near enough that his pine-and-fresh-rain scent wrapped around her, invading her nostrils. Since not breathing wasn't an option, she had no choice but to inhale him, dragging him into her lungs. She remembered how his sex-dampened skin tasted on her tongue.

Damn.

Shaking her head to rid her mind of those thoughts, she murmured, "What are you talking about?"

"You're too intelligent not to have researched the company. You had to know there'd at least be a chance I would attend the interview. Ambushed, Mycah. That's what I felt. But was that your plan? What would've happened if you hadn't been offered the job? Would blackmail have been the next step?"

Outrage scorched a path from her stomach up to her throat, temporarily incinerating her ability to speak. Hurt fueled the flames. She didn't deserve that—she *didn't*. And damn if she'd take it.

"You're correct," she said quietly, straightening her shoulders. "I did research Farrell International. But I didn't need to do any regarding you and Kenan Rhodes. I was well aware of who you both were since the media has covered you ad nauseam over the last three months."

The anger continued to simmer inside her, and maybe it fed a vein of recklessness as she shifted forward, eliminating even more space between them. Something flickered in his eyes, but he hid it behind a hooded expression before she had a chance to decipher it.

"I've apologized for not being truthful in the interview, and I'll do it again if you need me to. I'm sorry. But I won't apologize for some imaginary extortion plot that I had no intention of carrying out. I don't know whether to be offended or flattered that you've given me credit for something so ingenious. Criminal and devious, but ingenious, just the same." She tapped her bottom lip, narrowing her eyes. "Oh, wait. Offended." Then, she leaned into his space, cocking her head, and refusing to allow the anger or the pain to reverberate in her voice. "Why do I have the feeling that I'm once again being punished for the actions of another woman?"

His nostrils flared, and this time she had no trouble cracking the mystery in his gaze. Because it mirrored the same emotions zigzagging through her. For a second, she almost regretted her question. Almost lifted her hand to cup his lean cheek, tell him she didn't mean to pry, to forget she asked.

Almost.

But if he could lob bombs, then so could she. And she would be lying *again* if she claimed not to want the answer.

Not that she expected him to give it to her.

Besides, if he offered her an explanation, she might be expected to tender one in return. And damn if she was going there.

"You came looking for me for a reason, Mycah. I'm

beginning to suspect everything you do has an agenda. So get on with it, because I have work to get back to. What do you want?" he rumbled, taking a step away from her.

She detested that one step felt like a rejection.

A slap.

"I didn't want…this," she said, waving a hand back and forth between them. Suddenly she was tired. And sad. So inexplicably sad.

"I could've saved you a trip." He turned away, striding back behind the desk. For a moment, he studied the monitors in front of him, a frown creasing his brow. As if she'd been forgotten, dismissed. But he glanced up at her, his blue-gray gaze pinning her to the spot. "When I didn't say anything at your interview, that was me agreeing to never bring up our past—how did you put it?—*association* again. Believe it or not, I understand your reasons for not being honest. I get it. I also get that you want to make sure what happened between us in the past stays there. No slap and tickle with the boss. Got it. My mother was a waitress who worked twelve-hour shifts on her feet in a diner delivering food to truckers who thought her ass was on the menu along with the steak and eggs. And then, as if dodging handsy customers wasn't enough, she had to deal with bosses who believed she was fair game because she was a single mother who desperately needed that job. So no, you won't be getting that shit from me." He arched his eyebrow. "So if that's it?"

Only a fool would think he was inviting more conversation. And while a number of things could be attributed to her—liar, masochist, walking ATM—fool wasn't among them.

Nodding, she pivoted on her heel and exited the office. What else could she say? He'd nailed why she'd approached him—to establish a working boundary for them.

And yet...

Yet she left feeling as if gauntlets had been cast down and swords drawn.

Why did she sense this would be war?

Six

"How's the second semester shaping up, Angel?" Mycah asked her sister, leaning back in her chair as Beth, one of her parents' staff, ladled lobster bisque into her bowl. Mycah murmured her thanks at the young blonde. Picking up her spoon, she nodded, smiling at her little sister. "Last time we talked you were telling me how much you were enjoying your computer science class. Is that still going well?"

Angelique quickly patted her mouth with her cloth napkin, beaming at Mycah. "I am *loving* it! Ms. Ferrara is amazing and I'm learning so much from her." Angelique leaned forward, dark brown locs almost skimming the lobster bisque as she gushed over her favorite teacher. "And guess what?" she nearly squealed. Not allowing Mycah time to speculate, she charged ahead.

"We're developing our own computer games! How cool is that, right? Ms. Ferrara said colleges and future employers will look at our portfolio of games as evidence of our design ability, so high school is the perfect time to begin building it. We're going to download the Unity engine—"

"Angelique, please," Cherise Hill interrupted, a slight snap in her voice even though she didn't raise it. A lady never, *ever* raised her voice. That was a sign of poor manners and upbringing. As was vulgar language, laughing too loudly and showing up to an event uninvited. "Eat your dinner before it gets cold. Now, Mycah," she said, an ingratiating warmth infiltrating her words as abruptly as a light switch being flipped, "this is the first time you've had dinner with us since you started working at Farrell International. Our feelings have been a little hurt that you haven't been by to tell us about your new job."

Irritation crept through Mycah, and she tightened her grip on her spoon. She saw the embarrassment and pain that flashed across her sister's face before she bent her head, her locs swinging forward. Mycah shot her mother a glare, a hot rebuke burning the tip of her tongue, but at the last instant, she extinguished it. Not only would Cherise deny how dismissive and hurtful she'd been to her youngest daughter, but bringing attention to her bad behavior would only mean negative consequences for Angelique. Consequences Mycah was very familiar with—arctic silent treatments, ostracism or cutting criticisms.

No, if she could help her sister avoid that, at least for tonight, then she would.

Her heart ached with a yearning to reach across the table and pull Angelique into her arms. She crossed her ankles to keep herself seated.

"Well, starting with a new company, becoming acclimated to the culture there and learning my responsibilities, has been a little time-consuming. But in my defense, you haven't shown an interest in my job in the past. I didn't think you would be interested now."

Yes, it was a dig. One she should've been above. But she wasn't.

"That was before you started working for Cain Farrell," her father said from the head of the table.

Laurence believed in coating shit in sugar and talking out both sides of his mouth with other people, but not with his daughters. With business associates or guests at the endless parties he and Cherise attended, those dark brown eyes would glimmer with humor. But with his daughters, that gaze sliced with the precision of a surgeon's scalpel, exposing insecurities, faults and failures.

In spite of her employment helping to maintain their lifestyle, apparently, her job only *now* had any worth because of Cain. Because the Farrells were Boston royalty. If the Hills were considered earls or viscounts, then the Farrells were powerful dukes. And Mycah had suddenly become her parents' "in" to that rarefied circle.

Unease swirled in her belly like sour alcohol. She set her spoon down beside her bowl.

"Have you met Cain Farrell yet?" her father demanded.

"Of course," she said, keeping her tone level. Revealing her disquiet to her parents would be like throwing bloody chum into shark-infested waters. "I interviewed with him."

"And?" Cherise raised a perfectly arched brow.

Mycah blinked at her mother. "And I got the position of vice president of operations."

"Being deliberately obtuse doesn't become you, Mycah," her mother said, ice dripping from each syllable. "I have one daughter who is wasting the money we're paying for that exclusive school by focusing on computer games. And when our other daughter—the one who is pushing thirty and is still unmarried and doesn't even have any prospects—finds herself in front of a single, handsome billionaire, all she cares about is a *job* instead of a potential husband."

"Do you understand the influence, the power, the business a match between you and Cain Farrell could bring to Hill-Harper Inc.?" her father asked.

Hill-Harper, a holding company that had been founded by Mycah's maternal great-grandfather, enjoyed a respectable, conservative reputation here in Boston and nationwide. But for someone who only visited the office two or three days a week and was more or less a figurehead, Laurence always sought more. More wealth, more connections, more renown. And he viewed his daughters as tools to achieve his goals. "For a woman who claims critical thinking as one of her best skills, you fail to see the big picture here. The

most advantageous picture. Fine, get your foot into the
door with this *job*. But that isn't the endgame. Cain
Farrell is."

Jesus Christ. Briefly closing her eyes, Mycah leaned
back in her chair. Silently counted to ten. Fifteen.
Stopped at twenty. Ticking off numbers wasn't going
to calm her when dealing with her parents.

Mycah inhaled a breath, held it, then slowly exhaled.
"One. I went to Farrell International to interview for a
very important position that would benefit my career,
not to scope out a husband. Two. Even if I weren't a professional, it would've been pretty difficult to flirt, hit on
or climb over the conference room table and sexually
harass Cain Farrell as his two half brothers were also in
attendance. And three—and perhaps most important—
Cain Farrell is engaged to Devon Cole. And has been for
months. Which you both very well know."

Cain's sudden fairy-tale-esque engagement to the
little-known Devon Cole had taken Boston society by
storm. Some people had doubted the relationship, giving
it mere weeks before Cain broke it off with the pretty
but unassuming woman who worked at a local community center. But three months later, they seemed as
in love as ever. Even more so.

Making her parents' assertion that Mycah romanti-
cally pursue Cain even more ridiculous.

"That little nobody?" Her mother waved a hand,
laughing, the tinkling sound all the more cruel because
of its beauty. "Please. He can do better. All he needs
are options."

"So you've met the famed Farrell bastards?" her father asked, a smile curling his mouth. A gleam entered his dark eyes, lines fanning out from the corners, and he barely noticed as Beth cleared his bowl. "What was your impression?"

The Farrell bastards.

God, she hated that stupid, disrespectful name. With a passion.

How high society had taken such glee in salivating over news of Barron Farrell's illegitimate sons. Achilles, a giant of a man with his long hair and tawny skin. Kenan, biracial, tall, with smooth brown skin, a close-cropped beard and a lean but powerful build. They both shared the same distinctive blue-gray eyes of all the Farrell men, though, including their brother, Cain.

"They were fine," she said flatly, trying to dissuade him from the topic.

"Frankly, I'm surprised he let them sit in," Laurence continued, not discouraged by her tone at all. He chuckled, and it held an ugly undertone familiar to Mycah. "I know Barron's will stipulated Cain had to keep those two on at Farrell International for a year, but to include them in business decisions? I can almost see Kenan Rhodes since his family actually runs a company, even though it's nowhere near the level of Farrell. But that other one?" He shook his head, his grin widening.

"The Feral Farrell?" Cherise chimed in. "All that long hair and that hideous beard? And have you seen how big and…coarse he is? I don't care if Cain stuffs him in a suit—he's not fooling anyone. He looks like a thug."

"Did that one speak in the meeting?" Laurence snickered, leaning back as Beth set down his plate filled with filet mignon, sautéed asparagus and risotto. "Or did he just grunt?"

Her mother's laughter joined Laurence's, and it pounded against Mycah like pebbles striking her skin. Anger brewed inside her chest, a raging storm gathering wind and speed. And underneath…currents of shame coiled. These were her parents. She wasn't responsible for their actions, for their snobbery. But that didn't stop her from feeling tainted.

Sullied.

You don't know him.

She wanted to hurl those words at them. To make them understand and see the intelligent man who could be tender yet defensive, sensitive yet guarded. She'd glimpsed those pieces of him even as he actively shut her out. And just from the shreds of information he let slip about his past—only to be surrounded by people like her parents—she didn't blame him for those rock-solid walls topped by barbed wire.

Hell, she had her own barriers designed to prevent others from getting too close. Because people, starting with her own parents, had taught her that when they did, it was with an agenda.

Yes, she had trust issues.

Scanning her parents' smirking faces, she didn't have to wonder why.

Shaking her head, she pushed back her chair and rose from the table. "If you'll excuse me," she said, setting her napkin next to her forgotten bisque.

"Where do you think you're going?" Laurence

frowned. "Dinner isn't over. And we're not finished talking to you about this new job."

"I'm afraid I am through, though." Mycah injected regret into her voice that was pure bullshit, but the alternative—revealing to her parents that their jabs at Achilles sickened her—wasn't an option. "I just remembered I have an early meeting to prepare for. I'll make sure to come by next week for dinner. I'll call you later."

Before they could object, she strode from the room, ignoring her father's strident calling of her name. Neither of them would pursue her. Not only would they refuse to grant their staff anything to gossip about, but etiquette would keep them in their seats. And nothing—not even a fleeing daughter—trumped etiquette.

Sometimes Mycah detested their devotion to manners.

Then sometimes she was grateful for it.

Like now.

Within moments, she accepted her coat from their butler and stepped into the frigid January night. She paused on the top step of the Back Bay mansion and breathed deep.

How sad was it that she didn't inhale the scent of crisp air as she walked away?

No.

All she tasted was freedom.

Seven

Achilles plowed his fist into the punching bag, sending it spinning away and swinging back. He struck it once more, the power singing up his arm and into his shoulder. He welcomed the vibration that carried a subtle, sweet burn. He sought it, chased it as he pummeled the bag again and again until his arms trembled with fatigue and sweat dripped off his face and bare chest.

The gym in Farrell International had quickly become Achilles's favorite area of the building, next to his office. In both places, he lost himself either in code or in the numbing exhaustion of exercise. He could lock himself away…lock everyone else out. Even Cain and Kenan.

Guilt flickered in his chest, and he smothered the

urge to rub at the spot, as if he could erase it like a smudge of dirt. If only it were that simple.

He scowled, stalking over to the weight bench where he'd left his towel and bottle of water. Snatching both up, he wiped off the perspiration and downed almost half the water. At seven o'clock at night, he had the place all to himself. After a long day at work, most of the employees champed at the bit to leave. Not him. He delayed going back to that luxurious penthouse that had come with the appointment of co-CEO. Luxurious and cold. Three months he'd lived there, and he still felt like a squatter. To be fair, though, he had no desire to be there.

The cavernous apartment with its floor-to-ceiling walls, fireplaces huge enough for a man his size to stand in, a kitchen that would make Emeril Lagasse weep in envy, a library that his mother would've wrestled Belle to get…

It didn't make sense that he could live in a place so huge and still battle claustrophobia.

Nine more months.

That had become his mantra.

Nine more months, and his promise to Cain would be fulfilled. And then he could return to his cabin. His life. His peace.

Twenty minutes later, showered and dressed in battered but comfortable jeans and a long-sleeved T-shirt, he moved behind his desk, his mind already focused on work. Not for Farrell, though. No doubt it violated about ten company rules, but he used his after-work hours when all the rest of the staff had gone home to return to his pet project—the one he'd been laboring on for over a year now.

A high-fantasy, open-world, action-adventure video game geared toward at-risk youth. With world building that was a cross between the inner city and Middle Earth, he aimed to challenge players, teach them teamwork, decision-making, discipline, problem-solving, to think outside the box.

Six months of that year had been working with a psychologist on Achilles's mission and figuring out what elements he needed to include in the game to reach the kind of youth he'd once been. The youth he'd met and lived with for two years while locked up. This game wasn't just a possible moneymaker for him; it was his passion. He didn't want to hear why it wasn't marketable. Or that while his ideals were laudable, they weren't realistic. That's why he hadn't told anyone about it.

He might now be a millionaire, living in a penthouse at the top of a high-rise, but that didn't expunge lessons learned from bullies' fists or slaps from his mother's boyfriends: No one cares how smart you are. Keep it to yourself.

Achilles sank into his chair, reaching for his mouse to bring up his programs on the three monitors on his desk. His fingers flew across the keyboard, and within minutes he became engrossed in the script.

"Hey, Achilles." A fist rapped the top of his desk, reluctantly dragging him out of the world of code. "I'm not above doing something completely immature to get your attention. We both know this."

Sighing, Achilles leaned back in his chair and met

an identical blue-gray gaze. Kenan smiled at him, dropping into the visitor's chair, his long legs sprawling out in front of him. Unlike Achilles, his half brother still wore a dark blue, beautifully tailored business suit that appeared as fresh as if he'd just donned it minutes ago instead of hours.

"What're you doing here?" Achilles asked.

Kenan heaved a theatrical, loud sigh. "Aging well before my time worrying about you. I'm too young and pretty for these lines of concern to be etched in my forehead." He circled a finger over the nonexistent wrinkles. "So I'm asking you the same question. What are you doing here so late?"

Achilles snorted. Both at the dramatics and the deflection. Kenan might be better at hiding his ambition and hunger behind his charm and magnetic smile, but the other man didn't fool Achilles. Demons pursued his younger half brother, too. Achilles just didn't know Kenan well enough to identify them by name.

"Working." He jerked his chin up at Kenan. "Your turn."

"I'm wrapping up a couple of things." Kenan cocked his head and studied Achilles through shrewd eyes that belied his smirk. "But unlike you, Jan, I don't make a habit of burning the midnight oil. What gives?"

"Jan?" Yeah, he was stalling, but still… What the hell?

"Y'know, Jan. Middle child. *Brady Bunch.* 'Marcia, Marcia, Marcia!'" he chanted in an impressive falsetto. "You exhibit classic middle-child syndrome." He returned to his normal voice with a wide grin. Holding up a hand, he ticked off each point with a finger. "Un-social behavior. I mean, instead of choosing an office on the executive floor with Cain and me, you purpose-fully chose to be down here in the basement in a closet."

"It's not the basement," Achilles muttered.

Ignoring him, Kenan continued, "Trust issues. In spite of Cain trying to include you in Farrell business and showing you he's trying to make an effort to build a relationship with us, you're as cold as a hundred years of winter." When Achilles arched an eyebrow at his *Narnia* reference, Kenan scowled. "What? I read. And third, and the one that will possibly get me thrown out of here on my really great ass, but I'm going to say it anyway..."

Kenan leaned forward, planting his elbows on his thighs, his gaze losing all hint of humor and trapping Achilles behind his desk. In this moment, Achilles sym-pathized with a butterfly mounted on a corkboard.

"You don't want to get too close to Cain and me. Hell, you probably have your plane ticket already bought for the one-year anniversary of the reading of the will when you can return to Washington. But whether you admit it to yourself or not, you want us as brothers. You're just afraid we won't want you back. Which is bullshit. Because we're not Barron. Or..." Kenan's mouth hard-ened, locking away whatever else he would've said, but the flint in his eyes remained. "Like I said, we're not Barron."

Achilles stared at him, stunned. And if he could move, then maybe he would've kicked Kenan out of his office as he'd predicted.

His brother's words echoed through him, pounding inside his head like hammers. He longed to lash out at Kenan, order him to mind his own business. To stay out of his. That DNA didn't give him the right to go digging around in his psyche or play armchair psychologist. Or better yet, to tell Kenan he didn't know what the fuck he was talking about. Not about the office. Not about trusting him or Cain. And damn sure not about wanting their love or brotherhood.

Achilles was doing them a favor by staying. Wasn't that enough? What more did Kenan want from him? It was all he had to give. All he was willing to give.

All he could afford to give, goddammit.

His breath roared in his head. It lifted and dropped in his chest.

Slowly, he straightened fingers that he hadn't even realized had curled into tight fists. And second by second, he deliberately relaxed his body. Only then did he dare to meet Kenan's steady gaze. He expected challenge or even smug satisfaction to be in that Farrell blue-gray gaze. Instead, a disarming and disquieting compassion greeted him.

Part of him would've preferred the smug satisfaction.

"I think somewhere in California, Dr. Phil is sighing in relief that his job is safe."

The corner of Kenan's mouth quirked, and he shrugged a shoulder. "He better keep an eye on that wife of his, though. Robin's hot." Standing, he stretched. "I'm about to head out. What about you? Are you going to be here much longer?"

Saying yes would only invite more unwanted analysis so he shook his head. "No, I'm going to shut it down in a few minutes."

"In that case, join me for dinner."

Well, shit. He'd walked right into that one.

As if reading his mind, Kenan grinned. "You would be doing me a favor. My parents called and nagged me about not coming home in forever. With you there, they wouldn't dare air dirty laundry in front of a guest. It simply isn't done." Something flashed in his eyes, there and gone before Achilles could decipher it, but the grin remained. "Say you'll be my beard."

"As tempting as that sounds—" A buzz echoed in the room, and Achilles glanced down, noting the flashing red light on the company IT help line. Looked like someone else was working late, too.

Kenan snorted. "Huh. Saved by the bell. Literally. If only I had that excuse." He gave Achilles a mock salute. "Talk to you later, Jan."

Kenan strode out of the office with a chuckle. Glaring after him, Achilles picked up the phone and jabbed the blinking button.

"IT."

"Oh, thank goodness. I hoped someone was still there."

Oh. *Fuck.*

He closed his eyes, pinching the bridge of his nose. God hated him. Had to. Otherwise, why would *that* voice stroke his ear?

"Hello?" Mycah asked. "Are you still there?"

Lowering his arm, Achilles gripped the receiver tighter. "Yes, Mycah. I'm still here."

Her soft gasp echoed across their connection. "Achilles?"

"It's me," he said, impatience sliding into his voice. "What do you need?"

He didn't miss her brief hesitation, and he fully expected her next words to be "never mind." But this was Mycah.

"My computer just made this weird buzzing noise, then the screen did this even weirder staticky thing. I rebooted it, and now I can't find the most recent copy of the document I was working on. And I'm trying not to panic."

Trying and failing, because he clearly caught the thread of it in her voice.

"I'll be right up."

"Wait."

He paused, listening to her agitated breath over the line. "What?"

"You can't..." She emitted a sound that landed somewhere between a cough and a groan. "...you can't just tell me how to fix it over the phone?"

"No, I can't." He barely managed to swallow his snort. "What's the matter, Mycah? You have a problem being in the same space with me?"

"Of course not," she snapped. This time he didn't bother containing the snort. "Fine. See you when you get here."

The line went dead, and for a moment, he continued to hold the receiver to his ear. A grim smile curved his mouth.

He must be a glutton for punishment.

Because he could most definitely accomplish the task remotely, and with any other employee, he would've fixed her problem that way. But at the thought of seeing her, slivers of excitement stirred to life in his chest for the first time in two weeks.

Definitely a glutton.

Achilles ground his teeth together as he tried to focus on the computer monitor in front of him. And not on the woman behind him. Which was damn difficult to do when her lavender-and-cedar scent taunted him with what he'd once tasted but could never allow himself to have again.

Next time, he didn't care if he had to text her a Power-Point. He wasn't coming up here to this office.

"What're you doing again?" she asked, leaning over her his shoulder.

Not breathing wasn't an option. Dammit. "Locating your autorecovery folder to see if your documents are in there." His fingers flew across her keyboard. It sounded simple, but there were multiple steps required. He worked in silence, and in minutes found the folder. "What are the names of the files?"

Mycah pressed closer, her lush hip brushing his arm. He locked down a growl and forced himself not to flinch from the glancing touch that had lust blazing a path straight to his cock.

Employee. She was his employee now.

Off-limits.

Besides, she'd made it perfectly clear that their night together had been an aberration. For him, it had been, too. Because he'd been looking for a one-night stand and instead it'd ended up being the most intimate, emotional connection he'd had with someone in a very long time. And if that wasn't sad as fuck, then he didn't know what beat it.

Sadder still because he couldn't wrangle control over this need for her, even knowing she was a liar.

And not because she preferred to keep their relationship professional.

He hadn't misled her when he'd said he understood her reasons. He also hadn't meant to reveal all that he had about his mother, yet it didn't change the fact that he did get it.

No, she was a liar about the *why*.

And the *why* was always the most important.

"Damn, you are good," she breathed. "Those right there." She tapped the monitor. "'Release Policies and Procedures.' 'Operations Agenda Quarter One. Grisham Inc.'" She exhaled and it ended on a short burst of laughter. "Thank you, Achilles. I was a nervous wreck thinking I would have to re-create all of those files."

"You're welcome." He quickly pulled up the documents, then opened and saved them. "You should be fine now."

Shoving back her chair, he rose, but a small, delicate hand on his forearm might as well as have been a steel manacle, it stopped him that effectively. He stared down at that slim, long-fingered hand with its neatly polished nails. Branded. The heat, the intensity—it dug past flesh and seemed to scar. He fully expected to see the imprint of her palm on his skin when she removed her hand.

Yet he didn't move.

Because masochist that he was, he enjoyed the pain of the burn.

"Achilles," she murmured, hesitated. Then, as if remembering she still touched him, glanced down and lowered her arm. Didn't matter. The phantom imprint remained behind. "I was just about to, uh—" she stepped back, rubbed her arms up and down "—order food. Would you like to have dinner?"

He stared at her. Noted that she wouldn't look at him.

"Doesn't dinner cross the professional line you've drawn?"

That brought her head up, those gorgeous curls falling away from her face. And when her espresso eyes narrowed on him, something like satisfaction flared bright inside his gut.

He recognized it.

Had experienced it often when he'd grown big enough to fight back. And win.

The light of battle.

"Not when we're just two colleagues sharing a meal," she said evenly, though her gaze clearly ordered him to fuck off.

Did it make him perverse to be delighted by that visual middle finger?

Maybe.

But it was probably the lesser of two evils.

The second evil being his hard dick kicking against his zipper.

"One, we can never be 'just two colleagues.' Not as long as I'm me. People won't allow that." He planted one hand on her desk, fingers splayed wide, and gripped the back of her office chair with the other. Leaning forward, he said, voice low, "And two, you're a much better actress than I gave you credit for if you can sit across from me, talk about office gossip over chicken Parmesan and pretend you don't know how it is to have me swallow your moan as I push inside your body." He slowly shook his head. "Sorry. I'm not that good an actor."

Her eyes dilated, the pupils nearly engulfing the irises. "So you don't need friends?" she asked.

"Not you."

She barely flinched at the blunt answer, but he caught it. And part of him—the part that hadn't been cauterized in that jail and by the equally harsh life lessons that followed—almost reached for her. Almost cupped her jaw and thumbed the patrician slope of her cheekbone.

Almost apologized, even knowing she, an illustrious Hill, didn't consider him worthy enough of the word *friend*.

"Do you need anyone?" Mycah murmured.

The *no* hovered on his tongue, abrupt and definite in his head. But he couldn't utter it. Because as loud as the *no* roared in his mind, a small voice whispered underneath that it was a lie.

"Achilles—"

"Oh, honey, I'm so glad I found you," a feminine voice purred.

Surprise rippled through Achilles, and he stiffened, shifting away from Mycah and glancing toward the office door.

Mycah's mother.

He didn't need an introduction for her identity to be confirmed. Even if he hadn't done a deep dive on Mycah after the interview, it would've required only one glance at the older woman to determine their relationship. Though instead of her daughter's riotous curls, she wore her dark brown hair ruthlessly straight, they shared the same oval-shaped, chocolate eyes, elegant facial features and wide, generous mouth. The same smooth, brown skin. There were subtle differences, too.

A calculating hardness in her mother's eyes that Mycah hadn't yet adopted.

Faint lines fanned out from the older woman's mouth, as if she spent an inordinate amount of time with it pursed in disapproval. Which was a shame.

One day, would Mycah wear the same lines? Carry identical shrewdness in her gaze?

He glanced at her, and a weight settled on his chest. So heavy he fought the urge to rub it away.

"Mom." Mycah briefly met his gaze, and he caught a flash of emotion that on anyone else he would've labeled concern. But that couldn't be right. Why the hell would she be worried about him? "What are you doing here? At my job?" she asked, an edge in her tone.

Her mother laughed, a delighted, charming sound that grated across his nerves.

"To see my daughter, of course. Is that any way to greet your mother? Your friend will think we're heathens." She strode farther into the office, her arms outstretched.

If Achilles hadn't been studying Mycah so closely, he might not have noticed her hesitation, but he did observe the pause before she crossed the room and briefly embraced her mother, air-kissing both cheeks, then stepping back.

"That's much better," her mother admonished, brushing at the shoulder of Mycah's pale green shirt. "Getting you to return a phone call is a minor miracle, so you left me no other choice but to come hunt you down." Then, as if remembering Achilles's presence, she switched her attention to him with a warm smile. "I'm sorry for just barging in and interrupting. I'm Cherise Hill, Mycah's mother. And you are?"

"Achilles Farrell."

Recognition glinted in her dark eyes, and unease crept down his spine. Instinct warned that his identity hadn't come as a surprise to her.

"It's a pleasure to finally meet you, Mr. Farrell. You and your family have caused quite a stir these past few months." She approached him, her arm extended.

His chest tightened, everything in him repelling at the idea of grasping that hand, but despite the rumors circulating about his nature, he did have manners.

Enveloping her hand in his, he lightly squeezed it, then released her. "It's nice to meet you, Mrs. Hill."

"Hmm."

She studied him, and manners or not, he returned the favor. He knew her type, had come in contact with it even before arriving in Boston. If she expected him to cower and fidget underneath that analyzing, patronizing inspection, well, life was full of disappointments. The days when he bent for any man or woman were long gone.

"Mom, I'm sorry you had to come all the way downtown. But what is it that you needed?" Mycah pressed, drawing Cherise Hill's focus away from him and back to her.

Why did he get the sense that she had that maneuver down to a fine art?

"Well, like I said, if you'd have returned my or your father's calls, you would've known that we are planning a dinner party for a week from tonight."

"A party," Mycah repeated, tone flat. She crossed her arms, and Achilles frowned at the gesture that didn't strike him as annoyed but rather reeked of self-protection.

"Yes, honey, a party." Flint slid into Cherise's voice. "And consider this your official invite. And you, too, Mr. Farrell." She whipped around, aiming another of those hostess smiles his way, the warmth of it belied by the hint of frost in her gaze. "We would absolutely love if you joined us."

"Mom—"

"Thank you. I accept."

The words leaped out of him before he could cage them or consider the ramifications. But he didn't rescind them. Even when he noted the flicker of satisfaction in Cherise's eyes.

Even when he caught the glint of disquiet in Mycah's.

A glutton.

He was most definitely a glutton for punishment.

Eight

Pride goeth before a fall.

Jesus, how many times had Achilles heard that from his grandmother while growing up? And she'd immediately followed it up with "Don't be like your mother."

Achilles snorted. God knows Natia Lee had enough pride to have a few proverbs written about her. And he'd adored that about her.

Sighing, he nodded a thanks to the driver, who'd opened the back door of the sleek black Lincoln town car. Another amenity Cain had insisted Achilles accept. This one he didn't mind having so much as the others. The drivers in Boston were another level of crazy. And he didn't relish taking his life in his hands by getting behind the wheel among them.

"Thanks, Dave. If I don't call by ten, assume they

have me trapped in the Sunken Place and send in reinforcements."

Dave snorted, closing the door behind him. "Will do. In the meantime, try not to scowl too much and remember bathrooms are for pissing, not the carpets."

Achilles snapped his fingers before smacking his forehead. "Damn. Thanks for the reminder. I almost forgot that."

They looked at each other and snickered. After bonding over Seahawks and Patriots football, classic rap music and old mafia movies, the older man had become a friend in the last three months. Dave gave him a small salute, then returned to the car, leaving Achilles to stare up at the imposing Back Bay mansion. Unlike the other brownstones on the street, the Hills' home was composed of a white, marble-like material that stood out like Cinderella among the other belles at the ball. Large, intricate bay windows adorned three stories and even he, who knew nothing about architecture, could tell a fine and skilled hand had paid loving attention to the detail on the building's facade.

He approached the iron gate that separated the sidewalk from the property, and a black-suited staff member stood there. To let the guests in and bar the undesirables from entering, Achilles mused. And as he neared the man, he still didn't know which one the Hills considered him.

Minutes later, when he handed another young man his long wool coat, resignation filled him. His pride had dug this hole, and now he had to stand knee-deep in it.

Three hours. He could get through three hours of small talk, drinks, dinner and mind-numbing boredom—

"Achilles."

He turned at the sound of his name and froze.

The air in his lungs stuttered, stalled. Hell, the air in the ornate lobby came to a halt, as if stunned into utter stillness.

Mycah.

He should probably turn away, stop staring. Stop devouring the elegant column of her neck and the bared length of her delicate shoulders revealed by the upsweep of her curls in a crown on top of her head.

Stop worshipping the beautiful mounds of her breasts that he could map blindfolded with his hands and lips. A black corset-style top lifted them, cinching in a waist that was already small and drawing attention to the feminine flare of hips that had his fingers flexing to grab, dig into…mark. The formfitting skirt molded to her gorgeous curves, thick thighs and strong calves. Impossibly high stilettos completed the stunning visage of a confident, sexy woman who could willingly and joyfully bring a man—or woman—to their knees.

Lust burned through him. He pulsed with it. And if chatter and laughter didn't echo down the corridor, he would have wrenched that tight skirt over her gorgeous hips, pressed her against the dark paneled wall and released it into her.

Goddamn, he hurt.

"Achilles." She neared him, the heels of those shoes clattering on the marble floor. "Thanks for coming. Are you…okay?"

Okay? No. Unless *okay* had suddenly become synonymous with *hard as fuck*. "Yes, I'm fine." Because he wasn't able to help himself, he flicked another glance over her, devouring her in one quick look that he hoped she didn't catch. "You look beautiful."

Her fingers fluttered across her bare neck, and he couldn't help remembering when his hand had been the only necklace she'd needed. Shit. He really needed to get himself under control.

"Thank you," she murmured. "You do, too."

He arched an eyebrow. "Beautiful?"

She met his gaze even though a tinge of red painted her cheekbones. "Yes."

They stared at one another, the air between them charged, vibrating with tension, riddled with unspoken words.

Never one who gave a damn about his appearance, for once, he'd listened to Kenan's browbeating and worn the slim-fitting black three-piece suit and ice-blue shirt and tie. He'd bound his hair back in a bun and, though he'd refused to cut his beard, he had allowed Kenan's barber to trim it. Spying the glow of appreciation and—a fist clenched in his gut—desire in Mycah's gaze, he was glad he'd put forth the effort.

"This must be our guest of honor."

The intrusion of the deep, cultured baritone dropped between them like the blast of an arctic wind after a balmy summer. Dragging his attention from Mycah, Achilles met the piercing hazel stare of a distinguished, tall, older Black man. Again, no introduction was necessary, although it would undoubtedly be forthcoming.

Laurence Hill, president of Hill-Harper Inc. Mycah's father.

And just like his wife, he sent a frisson of disquiet skipping down Achilles's spine. Something in the eyes. In the too-wide smile. In the too-welcoming tone.

Lies.

He glanced at Mycah, saw her shuttered gaze. This family was built on lies.

"Laurence Hill." Mycah's father extended his hand toward Achilles. "Welcome to our home. We're delighted you could attend our little party."

"Achilles Farrell. Thank you for inviting me," he said, accepting the hand, and as he'd done with Laurence's wife, he shook and released it as quickly as possible.

"Of course, of course. When my daughter told us she landed a job at Farrell International, we couldn't have been prouder. It's a company with a long history based on tradition and family. And family is everything, isn't it?" Laurence said.

The words were innocuous enough, but the voracious gleam in his gaze...

So this was what Achilles had to expect tonight. God, the rich. Rage and bile churned in his gut. But damn if he would reveal how this asshole angered him. That's what the man wanted. A reaction. Strip away the money, the lineage, the connections and nothing separated people like him from criminals in jail.

If they got a rise out of you—if they pinpointed your weakness—then they had you.

Well, fuck them back in County then. And fuck Laurence Hill now.

"Yes, family is important," he said, conjuring up an image of his mother and his grandmother to keep his voice even.

Without his conscious permission, another picture wavered in his mind. Of Kenan and him standing in the library of that Beacon Hill monstrosity Cain called a home, supporting their older brother as he purged an old wound about their abusive bastard of a father.

Family *was* everything.

"There you are, darling." Cherise Hill sailed up to their trio, beautiful in a gold cocktail dress. She threaded her arm through her husband's and smiled at Achilles. "Mr. Farrell, it's wonderful to see you again. Do you mind if we call you Achilles? After all, there are so many of you Farrells now. It could get confusing." She chuckled.

God, these people.

"Achilles is fine."

"Mom, Dad, if you don't mind, I'm going to give Achilles a tour of the house and introduce him to the other guests." Mycah mimicked her mother's hold and weaved her arm through Achilles's. "Excuse us."

Not waiting for their reply, she led him past her parents and down the corridor. They passed a curving staircase, a wide fireplace with a sitting area and several doorways that opened to luxuriously appointed, empty rooms. Tension emanated from her, and just as they paused in front of the entrance to a room filled with milling, formally dressed guests, she turned to him, tilting her head back and pinning him with a dark, unfathomable stare.

"Why are you here?" she asked, tone low, almost vehement. "Why would you come here tonight?"

He didn't pretend to misunderstand her questions.

"Because she didn't want me to."

Mycah blinked. Exhaled a breath that ended on a short, humorless chuckle.

"It amazes me how certain people continue to underestimate you," she said to herself, shaking her head. Then, pasting a replica of her mother's hostess smile on her mouth, she waved a hand toward the room. "Ready?"

No. Not in the least.

"Lead the way."

Stepping into what Mycah had called a great room, he couldn't rid himself of the sense of being on display. He'd once accused Mycah of staring at him like he was an animal in a zoo. He'd been wrong. As he circled this room with Mycah guiding him from person to person, group to group, he sympathized with those caged beasts. Felt the weight of curious, assessing eyes. Heard the murmurs and whispers. The three months in society with his brothers had taught him how to hold his own with polite small talk, but that didn't make it any less suffocating.

And Mycah had remained by his side through it all.

That had surprised him. He'd expected her to make a few introductions then leave him to mingle as she knew far more people in attendance than he did. But she didn't. She'd stayed glued to his side, refusing to abandon him.

The last person who'd done that had been his mother, when he'd been in jail.

He jerked his thoughts from going down that road.

He might be thankful to Mycah in this moment, but she had nothing in common with his mother. Nothing in common with him. They were from two different worlds. Wanted different things. All he had to do was look around this house to see what was important to her, to her family.

All of which he wanted nothing to do with.

"Does that happen often?" Mycah asked, passing him the whiskey he'd requested from the bartender.

"What?" He accepted the drink, sipping the amber alcohol and welcoming the burn it left in his throat and stomach.

"That." She dipped her head toward the small group of men they'd just left. "When you meet people, they use the opportunity to engineer a meeting with Cain or extract information about him."

He considered her over the rim of the tumbler, taking another sip. "Often enough." All the time.

"It pissed me off. As if your whole identity is comprised of being Cain Farrell's brother." Her full, sensual mouth thinned. "As if you're not a brilliant software developer and designer in your own right who was courted by one of the most popular and successful computer systems design companies directly out of college. You've won numerous industry awards and cash prizes that total more than five million dollars. Hell, you were a millionaire before you even arrived in Boston. But they don't bother to learn that about you. All they care about is your last name and who your brother and father are," she fumed, fingers fisting her wineglass.

Achilles stared at her, shock ricocheting through him.

"You've done your research."

She glanced away from him, shrugging a slim shoulder. "My sister, Angelique, is a computer science whiz. When she discovered I worked with you, she might've raved about you. Fair warning. My parents didn't allow her to attend this party, but I can't promise she might not crash it anyway just to meet you. I'm not saying she's a stalker, just very enthusia—"

"Mycah." He pinched her chin between his thumb and finger, turning her head back to him. Her lips parted, trembled, and heat flashed in her dark eyes. "Thank you."

"For what?"

"For wanting to defend me." The corner of his mouth quirked. "With information received from your stalker little sister."

Mycah laughed, and he chuckled with her.

"Achilles, Mycah. Dinner is ready to be served." Cherise appeared next to them, her gaze zeroing in on his hand still gripping her daughter's face. He slowly released Mycah, turning to meet her mother's narrowed eyes. "As our special guest, we've reserved a place of honor at our table for you."

Achilles didn't trust that smile or the cold gleam in

her eyes. And forty-five minutes later, he knew he'd been right to trust his instincts.

The "place of honor" was a seat at the far end of the table stuck between the gallery owner with several failing shows on his left and the aging society maven on his right... Or the maven would've been on his right if Mycah hadn't insisted on switching with her much to the barely contained fury of her parents. Achilles hadn't been privy to the brief but furiously hushed conversation, but from the glares they'd shot his way, Laurence and Cherise had placed the blame of their daughter's etiquette rebellion squarely on his shoulders.

"So, Achilles, tell us," Cherise said, her voice clear and loud in the sudden silence of the dining room. Over twenty-five pairs of eyes focused on him, and though frigid skeletal fingers crept over his skin, he calmly met her gaze. "How are you enjoying Boston? It must be so different from...Seattle, is it? That is where you're from, right?"

Achilles set his spoon down next to the chocolate cherry mousse that had been set in front of him moments earlier and centered his attention on Cherise. Because only a fool didn't direct all his focus on a snake when he came face-to-face with one.

"I was born and raised in Seattle, yes, but I've lived in Tacoma for the past few years. As far as Boston, it's a beautiful city. Same as Seattle. They have their similarities. Some differences, too."

"Similarities?" Laurence chuckled, surveying his guests as if polling them. "How so?"

"Both cities have a lot to offer as far as culture, arts

and business. Their histories are different but proud and they're rich in ethnically diverse neighborhoods. Classism exists, but for the most part, at least from my experience, the people are the heart of each city."

Only a lone uncomfortable cough from somewhere to Achilles's left broke the thick silence. Even from the length of the long dining table, he caught the tightening of Laurence's mouth and the flash of anger in his hazel eyes. But then he laughed again, leaning back in his chair.

Beside Achilles, Mycah stiffened, the cadence of her breath shifting. Almost as if she were warning him. But he didn't need her to caution him.

Italian suit or orange jumpsuit. Glenlivet or Wild Irish Rose. Socioeconomic differences didn't matter. Predators were predators. He'd been educated long ago on how to handle them.

And he'd graduated with honors.

"Still, this must be all so new to you. This world. *Our* world." Laurence waved a hand, gesturing toward the crystal chandeliers suspended above the table, his bejeweled guests. "Correct me if I'm wrong, but wasn't your mother a...waitress?"

Rage poured through him. When Laurence had said "waitress," the connotation had been synonymous with *prostitute*. The bastard had said it that way on purpose, seeking a reaction from Achilles. No doubt attempting to get the Feral Farrell to make an appearance for his guests. And from the low murmuring around the table—not to mention the smug smile Laurence didn't even try to hide—they were eating it up.

"Dad, this isn't—"

Achilles closed his hand over Mycah's.

"Yes, my mother was a waitress," Achilles said, none of the fury that roared inside him evident in his tone. "Just as your great-grandmother was a domestic. And your grandmother—" he glanced at Cherise "—was a server in a speakeasy." He ignored the gasps that echoed in the room and deliberately picked up his spoon and slid a serving of mousse into his mouth. He paused and savored it as if the dessert was the most delicious thing he'd ever eaten, but in reality, it tasted like a mouthful of ashes. "They were admirable professions that all three of us should be proud of because of the women who worked hard to provide for their families and made sure they didn't go without."

"Damn," Mycah whispered next to him.

Yeah, Achilles silently snorted. Damn. Computers were his life, and there wasn't anything he couldn't do with them—or find on them.

"There's a big difference between your waitress mother and our ancestors, isn't there?" Cherise sniped, anger threading through her voice. "What happened with Barron Farrell? She must've thought she hit the jackpot when she met him. And yet she ended up stuck in some truck stop. Abandoned."

"Mother," Mycah snapped from beside him. "What the hell?"

Cherise gasped. "Mycah, excuse me?"

"No, I won't. Achilles is a guest in our home."

A sneer curled her mother's mouth, curdling her beauty into something spoiled, ugly. "Oh, please—"

"My mother was a single parent who worked her fingers to the bone to provide for her son. Because she loved me. She died still working and doing what I'd witnessed her do all my life—sacrifice so I could go further, do more, be better. She was the best person I've ever known. Did she believe she'd hit the jackpot with Barron? I don't know, since she never told me who he was and to my knowledge never received a check from him. Would she have liked to live like this?" He mimicked Laurence's earlier gesture and waved a hand toward the lavish room.

Meeting Cherise's and then Laurence's gazes, he compared them to parasites. Insects feeding on the labor, the sweat, the dignity of those they considered beneath them. Getting bloated until there was nothing left, and then preening as if they hadn't left destruction and carcasses in their wake.

"Possibly. Probably," Achilles continued. "But there's another difference between you and my mother. She didn't understand generational wealth or privilege. She didn't comprehend reaping the benefits of someone else's hard work simply because of the coincidence of birth and DNA. She believed in the efforts of her own hands and the satisfaction that comes from a hard day's work. So yes, maybe she might have enjoyed your beautiful home and your seven-course dinner—because she always loved great food—but I don't know if she would've stayed long in your world. She wouldn't have been content with being kept."

A silence so deafening rang in the room, it assaulted his ears. No one moved. Not even the servers, who stood behind the guests, their carafes of coffee frozen aloft in their hands. The stone of the mountains around his home possessed softer facades than Laurence's and Cherise's faces. That same flint hardened their eyes and Achilles didn't flinch from it. No, they'd sought to humiliate him, to tear down his mother in front of their guests. Undoubtedly, he'd made enemies of the Hills tonight, but he couldn't find a single fuck to give.

"We're ready for coffee, please." Cherise nodded to her staff, dismissing Achilles.

Or pretending to. The angry, stiff set of her shoulders contradicted her attempt to resume normal dinner conversation.

Everything in him demanded that he abandon this house and this farce of a party. He wasn't wanted, had never been anything but the planned entertainment, like a tragic circus clown. But pride kept his ass in the chair. Damn if they would run him from the table. He would stuff down the rest of this tasteless mousse and pretend just like them. Pretend that he belonged. Pretend that his skin didn't itch with the need to tear this suit off like the costume it was.

Pretend that all eyes weren't on him, watching, waiting...judging.

"Achilles." Mycah laid a hand on his thigh under the table, and the muscle bunched so tight, it ached. "I'm sorry."

She was part of this world. Belonged here. And yet, dark heat radiated from under her palm. He hated his body in this moment. Detested that it responded even when his heart, his head wanted nothing to do with this place—with her.

"Let it go," he ordered, shifting away, dislodging her touch.

He didn't need her apology. Or her pity.

After another excruciating twenty minutes, he finally stood from the dinner table and escaped into the drawing room with everyone else. But he didn't stay. He'd done his penance for the evening.

Past caring what the Hills or other members of Boston society thought about him, he slipped into his coat in the foyer, not bothering to wish his hosts good-night. They could forgive him or not. Most likely not.

Again. Didn't give a damn.

And as he strode out into the January night, preferring to wait out on the curb in the frigid winter cold for Dave rather than spend another second inside that mausoleum of a house, he swore that would be the last time.

The last time he returned to this house.

And the last time he gave a damn.

Nine

Anger was a wonderful motivator. Shame a close second.

Enough of a motivator to walk out on the rest of her parents' dinner party, bear the brunt of their outrage, brave the freezing January night and the judgy eyes of this security guard.

Wasn't the security for multimillion-dollar buildings supposed to be of the see-nothing, hear-nothing variety? After hesitating too long, he picked up the phone and punched in numbers on the keypad.

"I'm sorry to disturb you so late at night, Mr. Farrell, but this is John Ward at the security desk. There is a young lady here asking to see you. A Mycah Hill." He paused, suspiciously eyeing Mycah as he nodded, listening to whatever Achilles said on the other end.

"Right. I'll send her up, then. Thank you, sir." The guard hung up. "If you'll just enter your information here and sign in."

Mr. Ward slid a black registration book toward her and flipped it open to a clean sheet, setting a pen on top. Moments later, she followed him to a bank of elevators. He slid in a key card to a private car off to the side and a pair of doors opened. Stepping forward, he pressed a button, and shifted aside, motioning for her to go inside.

"This will take you to the penthouse. Good night, Ms. Hill."

With that, the doors closed, and she rode thirty-two floors. In seconds, the doors opened once more, and she came face-to-face with Achilles.

It'd been less than an hour, but it might as well have been days. The impact of him slammed into her like a cudgel to the chest. He'd removed his suit jacket and tie, but the ice-blue shirt remained, and the black vest hung open over his massive chest, and the slim-fitting pants clung to his hips and powerful thighs. The hem broke over his bare feet.

God.

Why did the sight of his bare feet reverberate through her like two cymbals crashing together? Maybe because it reminded her of the man and the intensity, the raw strength barely leashed beneath the civility of the suit?

Maybe. Did it matter when her nipples tightened under the cups of her corset top and her sex swelled and dampened beneath her skirt? When her belly tightened, as if in hunger, but not for the dinner her parents had served nearly an hour earlier. Only the man in front of her could sate her.

She inhaled, swerving her gaze away from him, over his shoulder. To the relative safety of the apartment behind him. It served to distract her, because *good Lord*. She was used to wealth, but this... Just the glimpse of the expanse of glass, marble and stone had her softly gasping in amazement.

Achilles shifted to the side, silently inviting her in. He didn't speak, just slid his hands into the pockets of his suit pants and trailed her as she wandered into the penthouse, gaping—yes, gaping—at the home that made her parents' home look like a hovel. Okay, maybe not a hovel. But definitely a single-family home.

Three glass walls invited the dark sky and Boston skyline into the apartment, granting the illusion of living among the clouds. Floating, freestanding structures separated rooms into different living areas—couches, a white piano, fireplaces, a chrome dining table, random sitting areas with low-slung furniture designating the purpose of the rooms. A steel and veined marble state-of-the-art kitchen encompassed the back end of the penthouse, while a suspended, curving, glass-encased staircase led to the second level.

She jerked her awed glance from her surroundings to Achilles. His mouth twisted into a caricature of a smile.

"Go ahead and say it. I'm a hypocrite."

She blinked. "What?"

"Lecturing your parents on excess and benefiting from the work of someone else and living here." He

Get up to 4
FREE FABULOUS BOOKS
You Love!

To thank you for being a loyal reader we'd like to send you up to 4 FREE BOOKS, absolutely free.

Just write "YES" on the Loyal Reader Voucher and we'll send you up to 4 Free Books and Free Mystery Gifts, altogether worth over $20, as a way of saying thank you for being a loyal reader.

Try **Harlequin® Desire** books featuring the worlds of the American elite with juicy plot twists, delicious sensuality and intriguing scandal.

Try **Harlequin Presents®** Larger-print books featuring the glamourous lives of royals and billionaires in a world of exotic locations, where passion knows no bounds.

Or **TRY BOTH!**

We are so glad you love the books as much as we do and can't wait to send you great new books.

So don't miss out, return your Loyal Reader Voucher Today!

Pam Powers

LOYAL READER
FREE BOOKS VOUCHER

YES! I Love Reading, please send me up to 4 FREE BOOKS and Free Mystery Gifts from the series I select.

Just write in "YES" on the dotted line below then return this card today and we'll send your free books & gifts asap!

➡ ----- YES ----- ⬅

Which do you prefer?

☐ **Harlequin Desire®**	☐ **Harlequin Presents® Larger Print**	☐ **BOTH**
225/326 HDL GRGA	176/376 HDL GRGA	225/326 & 176/376 HDL GRGM

FIRST NAME   LAST NAME

ADDRESS

APT.#   CITY

STATE/PROV.   ZIP/POSTAL CODE

EMAIL ☐ Please check this box if you would like to receive newsletters and promotional emails from Harlequin Enterprises ULC and its affiliates. You can unsubscribe anytime.

HD/HP-520-LR21

wore that same dark smile. "I believe that makes me the definition of a fraud."

"Since a fraud or a hypocrite would be the last persons to admit they were as much, I doubt it." She tilted her head. "Let me guess. Cain?"

His eyes narrowed on her, and she chuckled, shaking her head.

"It's not difficult to guess. Kenan is from Boston. You relocated to Boston and wouldn't have had a place to stay. And unknown half brother or not, Cain wouldn't have had you living in a place he wouldn't live in himself. And this place—" she pivoted in a small circle, again taking in the glass palace in the sky "—has Cain Farrell written all over it."

"And what has me written all over it?"

She knew a challenge when she heard it. Knew when she was being set up for failure, too.

"Keep some of the glass and the sky. More walls. Less steel and chrome and all the amenities. I don't think you mind the fireplaces, but not gas. I think..." She paused, cleared her throat and considered the wisdom of her next words, but what the hell? "I think you're like how you described your mother tonight. You like to see the product of your own hands. So you would want to chop your own wood for your fireplace. Which means trees, nature and not a glass castle on the thirty-second floor. How am I doing?"

He didn't answer, just stared at her with that bright gaze that both unnerved her and set her ablaze.

"Why are you here?" he rasped.

"To make sure you're okay."

Once more he studied her with that unblinking, measured scrutiny. Then, after a moment, he gave his head a hard, abrupt shake and stalked toward the living room. "Do you want a drink?"

"Since I skipped after-dinner drinks, definitely."

He glanced at her over his shoulder, eyebrow arched. "I'm sure that went over well."

She flashed him a dry smile. "Swimmingly. If you can call dire warnings of ruining my family's reputation by running after you like a common trollop—who even says *trollop* anymore, I ask you?—'well.' If so, then yes, it went over very well."

"That's...dramatic." He reached the built-in bar and removed a Sam Adams for himself from the fully stocked mini-refrigerator. "What can I get you?"

"I'll have what you're having."

He didn't comment on her choice, just twisted off the cap of his beer, handed it to her and retrieved another for himself. Only after she lifted the bottle to her lips for a sip and downed the ale, did he ask, "Why are you really here, Mycah?"

Slowly, she lowered the beer, met his piercing gaze.

To apologize for my parents' behavior.

To look you in the eye and see for myself that you don't despise me.

All true. All answers she could give him, and he would most likely accept them. All she had to do was say them. Just say them, dammit...

"Because I didn't feel safe in that house."

Oh, God. Why had she said that?

Lightning flashed in his eyes, and she wanted to hide from it.

She wanted to hurl herself at it. Be struck by it.

"And you feel safe here? With me?" he asked, a low rumble in his voice.

"Yes."

As inane as it was, as tumultuous as their past and current...relationship might be, she did. She harbored zero doubts that he'd ever intentionally hurt her, exploit her. If she'd come seeking shelter, he'd not only give it, he'd use his own body to provide it. That was his nature.

No.

It's who he was.

After witnessing the pettiness, the cruelty her parents were capable of tonight, she needed that haven. She craved that security. She'd come here on the pretense of making sure Achilles was okay, but really, she was the one who desperately wanted to be assured.

Did that make her a user? Did that make her selfish?

"Stop, and no."

She blinked, snatching herself from the downward spiral of her thoughts. "I'm sorry?"

"Wherever you were going right now in your head. You had a deer-in-headlights look in your eyes."

"I'm selfish. A user," she whispered.

"You're going to have to explain that one." He cupped her elbow and led her to one of the sitting areas, guiding her to a black armchair. "Sit. Because you look like you're about to fall over."

"I convinced myself I was coming here for you. When it was about me, *for me*, all along. Selfish," she repeated, tilting her head back to meet his gaze. "I came here to use you."

She expected his disgust at her admission. At the very least annoyance. Not that flicker of...*oh, God*, desire.

"Use me in what way, Mycah?" Another man might have hunkered down next to the chair, minimizing his size so she didn't feel towered over or intimidated. Not Achilles.

And she didn't feel intimidated or overpowered.

No. She felt covered. Protected.

And so aroused she could barely breathe without taking in his scent—pine, fresh rain and sex.

"Mycah."

"I want... I would..." She couldn't say it. Couldn't push it out.

In her family, asking for what you needed—other than the latest season's fashion line or the newest car—was akin to exposing your neck to an apex predator. It was revealing a weakness. When he'd been a stranger, someone she hadn't expected to see after a night together, it'd been easier. But he wasn't a stranger anymore.

If he'd ever really been.

And as much as she'd run to him tonight...as much as she trusted him not to intentionally hurt her... What this man could inadvertently do to her heart would make a natural disaster look like an April shower.

"We'll table it for now." He sank into the chair across from her, his sprawled long legs bracketing hers.

He didn't speak as he tipped the bottle to his mouth

and drank. And she did the same, watching him, mesmerized by the oddly sensual sight of his ale-dampened lips and the dance of his Adam's apple as he swallowed. Maybe it was the alcohol she'd barely sipped, but she longed for nothing more than to lean forward and slowly close her teeth around that strong throat and flick her tongue over his skin. Taste the earthy, salty flavor of it.

User, a small, smug voice rustled in her head. The apple didn't fall far from the tree.

"I'm sorry, Achilles," she whispered, tracing a fingertip through the condensation dotting the bottle. "You didn't deserve that kind of treatment tonight. I know you didn't want my apology earlier, but I need to offer you one. Or try to."

"Look at me."

She lifted her head, meeting his gaze, a flicker of annoyance at her immediate obedience to his order mingling with a flash of lust.

"I didn't want to hear it earlier because it wasn't yours to give. The same now." He leaned forward, setting his beer on the floor before propping his forearms on his thighs. Pinning his bright eyes on her, he said, "And yes, I was mad as fuck and trying to hide it with everything in me so I didn't end up giving your parents and everyone else at that table the satisfaction of proving I was who they believed. The beast. The thug. The Feral Farrell."

"You know about that?"

He snorted. "I'm not deaf or blind, Mycah."

"No, I know that." She waved her hand, frustrated. "I guess I hoped you hadn't…"

"My mother always told me, it's not what they call you, but what you answer to. Your parents or any of the people here in Boston don't define me." He paused, studied her, and she fought not to recoil from that incisive stare. Fought not to hide lest it perceive too much. Slice too deep. "So why are you allowing them to dictate who you are?"

"I'm not…" Damn him. She closed her eyes. Hiding. And not caring if he knew it. No, screw that. She reopened them, glared at him. "I told you before that you don't know me. So stop presuming that you do."

"Then tell me."

If he'd scoffed at her, she might've left. Might've ordered him to fuck off as she stalked out of there in righteous indignation. But his quiet offer full of curiosity, of genuine interest, deflated her anger.

Soothed her hurt.

"In the interview, Cain asked me why I wanted to work for Farrell. The answers I gave—promotion, opportunity, experience—all were true. But he asked the wrong question. It should've been why I *needed* to work there. Because I do. I *need* this job." She huffed out a laugh, holding the cold bottle between both of her palms and rubbing it back and forth, back and forth. "That party my parents threw tonight? Do you know who paid for it? Me. Or I will at the end of the month. Because the monthly allowance that they receive from Hill-Harper will be gone, spent on clothes, jewelry, lunches, spa appointments, gifts for their friends. And it will be up to me to cover the mortgage, household bills, staff salaries and any other outstanding debts they owe. See, my parents deride my career, but they depend on it."

"You're enabling them, and they're taking advantage because they know you'll pay their way." He growled, anger radiating off him. "That isn't love. That isn't sacrifice."

She shook her head. "It's family," she insisted. "If your mother—"

He slashed a hand through the air, cutting off her argument. "My mother would never have asked that of me. Which is why I would gladly have given her the world if she'd lived. And you know what she would've done, Mycah?" He leaned forward, his blue-gray eyes burning into hers. "Told me no. She would've fought me on it until I wore her down. C'mere." He crooked two fingers, beckoning her closer, and she slid forward on the chair cushion. "You don't even believe the bullshit you're telling me," he said, his voice impossibly gentle, brutally blunt.

Tears sprang to her eyes, stinging them.

But then, the truth tended to do that.

Sting.

"What is it, baby?" he whispered. "You're safe. Tell me."

The truth grappled with self-preservation in her throat for approximately five seconds before it burst from her.

"Three and a half more years. That's all I have left. Three and a half more years before my sister graduates from high school and goes to college. Then I'm free. I'm paying for her tuition, and I can't abandon her. She's brilliant, Achilles, and deserves the best education possible. I won't take that away from her, and I can't lose her. She's the only real relationship I have. I don't put it past my parents to prohibit me from seeing her if I stop paying their bills. But in three and a half years, she'll be through with high school and she'll be eighteen, an adult. And I'll have what I've dreamed about for years."

"What have you dreamed of, Mycah?" he pressed when she hesitated.

She threaded her fingers through her curls—or attempted to. Remembering too late the strands were secured in an updo, she clenched her hands tight before dropping them to her thighs.

"Mycah."

"Freedom." As the word echoed in the room, she winced, emitting a hushed, embarrassed chuckle. Turning, she set her neglected beer bottle on the side table. Anything to avoid looking at him. "Freedom," she repeated less vehemently, with a much heavier dose of self-deprecation. "You must think I'm dramatic."

"You think I don't understand the need for freedom?"

She jerked her head back to him, shock ricocheting through her.

He slowly nodded. "You know the terms of Barron's will. By now, everyone does. For most people, it would seem like a dream come true. Co-run a multibillion-dollar company. Instant billionaire. But I never asked for it. Never wanted any of it. And I'm counting down the months, the days until I'm out of here. Out of Boston. Until I'm free from it all."

He surged from the chair and strode to the window,

yanking the tie from his hair on the way. Burrowing both hands through the thick strands, he fisted them, yanking so hard, she winced in sympathy. He splayed his fingers wide on the sheet of glass. As if attempting to reach through it to the sky beyond.

"Do you know the reason I hate the name *Feral Farrell* so much?" he rasped. "Because a part of me fears that there's some truth in it. Sometimes I feel like I'm going crazy within the confines of this…world. After—" he broke off, his hand balling into a fist against the window, his head bowing between his shoulders "—I left Seattle, I deliberately chose a specific way of life for myself. A quieter life, a simpler one. This one… It's too loud. Too harsh. Too mean. I know Cain and Kenan think I'm pulling away from them, that I'm distancing myself from them, but I can't let myself become too attached because I can't stay here. They were both born here. This is home for them. I don't belong here."

She rose and went to him, unable to remain in her chair any longer. Without questioning the wisdom of what she was doing, she crossed the room and didn't stop until she stood behind him. So close, her forehead pressed into the indentation of his spine. So close, the toes of her stilettos nudged the bare heels of his feet. So close, her hands slipped under the edge of his vest and cupped his slim waist.

Achilles's body went rigid, but he didn't move away from her. Taking that as a positive sign, she closed her eyes, breathed him in. Dragged that decadent scent of the outdoors into her lungs and held on to it like a drug. Then as she exhaled, she already craved the next hit.

"You asked me how I wanted to use you," she murmured, her words puffs that fluttered against his vest. "I came here because I needed you to hold me. To touch me. To shield me from the world just for a little while before I have to go back out and face it again." She slid her hands over his stomach, up the ridged ladder of his abs until her palms covered his pounding heart. Turning her head, she pressed her cheek to his back. "I think we can give each other that. I don't see anything wrong with both of us using each other."

For the longest moments, he didn't stir. The *thump, thump* against her hand the only movement. But in a sudden explosion of action, he wrenched out of her embrace, turned and damn near leaped on her.

Excitement and lust combusted within her, and she met him in a clash of lips, tongue and teeth, his beard abrading her chin and mouth in a sensual caress. God, it'd been so long. So damn long since she'd been touched. No, that was wrong. Not just simply touched. So long since she'd been touched by *him*. By *Achilles*.

The whimper that escaped her throat should've embarrassed her, but she was beyond that. Tunneling her fingers through his thick, cool strands, she fisted them, dragging his head down so she could feast on the mouth that had been taunting her for weeks. Impatient and so damn hungry, she licked him, demanding he give just as much—no, more—in return.

His big hands gripped her head, angling this way. Then that way. Then this way again. As if he couldn't get enough. As if he'd never be satisfied. Join the club. He could suck at her tongue, nip at her lips, lick the roof of her mouth, and she would still yank on his hair, claw at his scalp, silently beg for everything.

This wasn't a kiss.

It was war.

And goddammit, yes, she wanted to be a casualty.

"This dress. It's been fucking killing me all night. How do I get you out of it?" he muttered against her mouth, his hands roaming her breasts, belly, hips.

Chest rising and falling on labored breaths, she turned, giving him her back. "Hooks at the back. Zipper at the hip." She glanced over her shoulder at him. "Hurry."

The next few moments were an exercise in patience as he worked his way through the delicate hooks of the corset-style top, but the brushes of his fingertips over her spine and the caresses of his coarse curses in her ears only heightened the rush of burning arousal in her veins. By the time the top loosened around her breasts and the skirt dipped around her waist, she trembled with lust, and gooseflesh pebbled her skin. And when he lowered the dress, the black material pooling around her shoes, leaving her clad only in a silk thong and thigh-highs, she sank her teeth into her bottom lip to imprison the sob of need that clambered at the back of her throat.

"Turn around." He paused. "Please."

That *please* in his gruff voice, with a note of the same need that burrowed through her, nearly sent her to her knees. Before she could do as he asked, though, he grasped her elbow.

"Wait."

He knelt in front of her, and the air evaporated from

her lungs. Her body and mind were of one accord as they both recalled the last time his face and that beautiful beard of his had been between her legs. But this time Achilles's attention wasn't focused on her sex but on her feet. Carefully, he removed her stilettos and swept the dress to the side. He sat back on his heels, staring up at her. Her body had never been the "perfect" size four, much to her mother's dismay. Even so, over the years, Mycah had come to not just accept but to love her body, regardless of others' opinions.

And as Achilles's gaze caressed her thighs, which had never been slim, her hips, which had always been rounded, her belly that had never been completely flat and her breasts, which had always been fuller than an A cup, she felt desired. Worshipped.

Perfect.

"You're beautiful."

Truth ran through his voice, in every syllable. And no matter what might pass between them elsewhere, here, in this, she believed him.

"You're overdressed." She hiked her chin toward him, arching an eyebrow at his shirt, vest and pants.

His hands went to his vest, and he shrugged free of it. When his fingers gripped the top button of his shirt, she sank to her knees. Lust pumped through her, hot and heady, as she brushed his hands aside and took over the task. With every slice of inked brown skin revealed, her arousal ratcheted higher. She squeezed her legs against the sweet pain in her sex, knowing her flimsy lacy thong hid none of the evidence of the desire dampening her upper thighs. And as she pushed his shirt from his shoulders, Achilles confirmed as much when he dipped a hand between her legs, stroking a fingertip across the skin just below her folds and lifted glistening fingers to his mouth.

Deliberately, he slid them between his parted lips, licking them clean. His dense, black lashes fluttered close, and he moaned, the sound ravenous. She whimpered, an aching tug pulling hard in response.

"Touch me," she pleaded, past pride. "Touch me, please."

His arm snaked up, hand cupping the back of her neck and hauling her forward. Their bare chests collided, his mouth covering hers. She tasted herself on him, and the faint musk enflamed her. She opened wider for his possession. He cupped her behind with both hands, squeezing, and she arched into his hold, loving how he told her without words how much he enjoyed her body. Adored her body.

Tearing her mouth from his, she trailed her lips over his jaw, down his strong throat. She paid special detail to the swirls, geometric patterns, lettering and biomechanical art covering his shoulder, arm and chest. He was beautiful, and she closed her eyes against the sting of tears. Silly. God, she was being silly.

"Mycah?"

He cradled her face. Or tried to. She dodged those big palms, ducking her head and flicking her tongue over his flat, brown nipple. His groan rumbled under her mouth, and she raked her teeth over the nub, then sucked it, drawing hard.

"Damn, baby." He carefully removed the band and

pins from her hair, then drove his hands through the curls, tangling his fingers in them, tugging, sending darts of pain scattering across her scalp. "Again. Do it again."

She complied. Gladly. Placing her palms against his wide shoulders, she lightly shoved. One of his muscular arms wrapped around her, and he fell back to the carpeted floor. She took swift advantage, crawling on top of his giant frame, straddling his abdomen and moaning deep as those ridges pressed against her wet, swollen folds. Another moan rolled out of her, and she couldn't have stopped herself from grinding against him if inhaling her next breath depended on it.

Why did she need to breathe when pleasure so intense was turning her into living ecstasy?

"No?" Achilles growled, circling her neck, applying just enough pressure to have a dark, erotic wave swirl through her lower belly and pool between her legs.

"Yes," she damn near whined, leaning into his hold. Another buck of her hips, another, and another, and she shuddered, so close to coming just from grinding over him and that illicit grip on her throat.

How was that possible?

Because it was Achilles.

"I don't want to want you." He accompanied the admission with a sweeping caress of her nipple.

Electricity sizzled in her veins, the sparks echoing in her head, but she still clearly heard him. And underneath the pleasure, hurt vibrated within her. She lifted her hand, preparing to shove him away from her breast, but when he pinched the tip, tweaked it, her hand fell away. She surrendered to the pleasure even as she couldn't escape his words.

"You're everything I told myself I shouldn't have. Everything that's destructive to me. And yet—" he cupped her, levered up and sucked her into his mouth, his tongue licking and circling her flesh before crushing a kiss to her lips "—you've become my fantasy."

"And you hate us both for it," she whispered against his lips.

He stared at her, his wolf eyes so bright, so intense it almost hurt.

"Yes. Almost."

A pain carved into her, sharpened by the tender care he gave her. She wanted to hate him back, to strike out at him for making her care. This was sex. Ill-advised sex, at that. Nothing more. But her pounding heart whispered *liar.*

Good thing her heart held no power over her head, just as only her body could rule her for tonight.

Breaking the kiss, she slid down his body, scattering kisses down his torso, her fingers grasping the tab of his pants, undoing them, then tugging down his zipper. Scooting farther down, she settled in the vee of his thighs and fisted his cock. His guttural growl broke on the air, and satisfaction flooded her. He might hate desiring her, but his dick didn't. This part of him— she freed him from the confines of his black boxers— loved her.

She didn't waste time teasing him. Not when his dense, earthy musk teased her, and her mouth watered for the taste of him. Arrowing his length downward, she swallowed him. Another of his harsh moans rippled through the room and two large hands cradled her head, oddly gentle, and a contradiction to the barely leashed control of his straining body.

Closing her eyes, she lost herself in him. The feel of him sliding over her tongue. The threat of him nudging the back of her throat. The power of him pulsing in her hand. The taste of him she coaxed on each glide back up the length of his cock.

In this moment, as he bunched her curls in his hands, lifting them away from her face so he could glimpse every hard suckle, she was…powerful. He was hers.

And she was his.

In this moment.

"Enough." His gravel-roughened order came seconds before he grabbed her by the shoulders and hoisted her up and off his body. But only long enough to shuck his pants, remove a condom from the wallet and sheathe himself. Then he reached for her, pulling her back on top of him. Grasping one of her hips with one hand, he squeezed his cock with the other, holding himself at her entrance. "Take me, Mycah."

It could've been a demand. It could've been a plea.

She gave in to both.

Slowly, she sank down over him.

Her breath snagged in her throat at the impossibly tight fit, and she paused, shaking. Yes, she'd done this with him before. But this position made him seem bigger, thicker. Her fingernails dug into the dense muscles of his chest, and she shook with the increasing pressure as she pushed down, taking more.

The stretch. The burn.

And underneath? The pleasure.

Pleasure, simply because it was Achilles inside her, filling her, branding her flesh, marking her.

"Shh. Easy, baby. Take what you need." He cupped her breasts, whisking his thumbs over the beaded nipples, his long hair tangled around his head. His hooded gaze seemed to miss nothing—not her struggle, not even her pleasure. His face hardened into a mask of such fierce lust, it stole what little air she had left in her lungs. "You're so fucking tight. So wet. Months I've been dreaming about this, and nothing came close to how perfect you are."

Months? So she hadn't been alone in not forgetting that night?

A silent cry echoed in her head, and she sank lower. Oh, God. She had to move. Had to...do *something*. Using his chest as leverage, she rose off him until just the tip of him kissed her folds, then she took him back inside, the wide, thick length of him claiming her just as she claimed him.

Twin ragged groans penetrated the room, and with his hands still caressing her breasts, she rode him. Cautiously, at first, but gradually, with more abandon until he filled all of her and her behind slapped his thighs. It was so damn *good*.

Achilles replaced his hands with his mouth, drawing on her, sucking on her, torturing her as his big hands encouraged her to fuck him...to break him.

He tunneled a hand into her hair, pulled her head

down as he reached between them and circled a blunt fingertip over the nub of flesh at the top of her sex.

"Let me feel you come all over me, baby."

This was all demand. And she obeyed. He gave that engorged, pulsing flesh two more hard, relentless circles and she exploded, came apart for him. For herself.

And as he followed close behind her, his giant body surging and pitching beneath her, she clung to him, wringing out every last bit of the orgasm snapping through her like the hottest of lightning bolts.

Just like this release, she would claim all of tonight for herself because tomorrow she had to start the process of letting go all over again.

"Will you tell me about her?"

Beneath her, Achilles's body jerked, then stilled, as if he hadn't meant to betray his reaction to her question but hadn't quite managed to hide it. His heart beat solidly, but at an elevated rate under her ear.

They continued to lie in his bed, the sheets twisted around their bodies from their last bout of sex. At some point during the night, he'd carried her from the living room up the stairs to the bedroom, and she'd discovered once more that slow, tender sex with Achilles was just as hot and mind-blowing as when it was fast and intense. But now, as the sweat dried on their skin and her thoughts had started whirling again, she couldn't stop them.

And couldn't keep them from tumbling out of her mouth.

Mycah didn't repeat the request or say anything else

to expound on the *her*. She didn't need to; they both knew to whom she referred.

He remained silent so long, she assumed he decided not to answer her. Disappointment flashed inside her chest, but not surprise. Sex didn't mean he would suddenly confide in her. Especially about someone who'd obviously had such an impact on his—

"What do you want to know?" The words erupted from him as if he'd propelled them out. Get them out or never say them at all.

She blinked, part of her unsure she'd actually heard him, but she quickly recovered, not willing to squander this opportunity.

"Are you still in love with her?" *Oh, for God's sake.* She mentally cringed. That's what she led with? Dammit, she sounded…needy.

"No." Gently grasping her shoulders, he lifted her. Sitting up, he slid across the mattress until his back hit the headboard. His hair tumbled about his face and shoulders, that piercing gaze narrowing on her. "Why would you ask me that?"

She shrugged. How could she answer that, when she didn't know herself? "When someone remains so angry with another person it's usually because they still have strong feelings for them."

"I'm not angry with her." His dark brows slashed down in a frown. "She taught me a valuable lesson I'll never forget, but I'd have to care about her to be angry. And I don't give a damn either way."

"What was the lesson?" Mycah whispered, certain she already knew.

He watched her for several long, quiet moments, then said, voice flat but soft, "Most rich women will toy with someone out of their tax bracket, but when it comes down to it, they're not settling for the dirty little secret."

Each word landed like a solid punch, and through sheer will she didn't flinch from the blows. Did he believe she saw him as a dirty secret? Second class? Out of her league? She scrolled through their interactions, beginning at the bar and ending with the evening at her parents' house. Here, in the living room with his confession about hating himself for wanting her.

Yes, he did believe that.

Pain and anger sizzled inside her, but as quickly as it flared, she extinguished it. This wasn't about her. And as much as she longed to defend herself, she couldn't make it about her.

"Will you tell me what happened?" she asked.

He cocked his head, surprise flickering in his eyes. "Why is it important to you?"

"Because I want to know who I'm being punished for. And why." And maybe, just maybe, though he claimed he wasn't angry, speaking about it could lance this obvious wound.

Again, he didn't immediately reply, but after a long pause, he finally nodded. Turning his head, he shifted his gaze from her to the glass wall that, during the day, would provide a phenomenal view of Boston Harbor.

"I met her not long after my mom died," he began. "My mom and I were living in Tacoma by then, and it'd been just us. You might not have noticed, but I don't play well with others—" a slight quirk of his lips, there and gone in an instant "—so I didn't have anyone among my coworkers that I'd call friends, just acquaintances. So with Mom gone, I was alone, and when this beautiful, sophisticated, cultured woman approached me at one of my company's investors' parties, I fell. And I fell hard."

Okay, maybe she didn't want to hear this story. Jealousy sparked and writhed inside her, and though she reminded herself she'd literally asked for this, she couldn't snuff it out. Couldn't abolish the thought of this *beautiful, sophisticated, cultured woman* with this virile, gorgeous man.

"She claimed to love me, said she was interested in my career, concerned about my well-being. Even encouraged me to see a grief counselor about my mother. But the moment the counselor cautioned me about jumping into a relationship so soon after Mom's death, she found a way to shut that down. Told me the counselor was against us. And stupid-ass me believed her. Fuck." He loosed a harsh bark of laughter. "I was so goddamn dumb and needy."

"Stop it." For the first time since he started relaying his story, she spoke, scooting closer and grabbing his hand in both of hers. He turned from the window, dipping his head to stare down at their clasped hands. "The fact that you recognized you needed a counselor is brave. You actually going? Even braver. That she manipulated you into stopping, using your trust and love to further her own agenda, is her shame, not yours. So don't you dare take that on you."

He lifted his gaze to hers. He didn't nod, but he didn't refute her, either. Mycah took that as a win.

"We were together a year and a half, although that was a year too long. In that time, I never met her family, although she promised I would, I just needed to be patient. She did take me around her friends, though. Bought me new clothes, dressed me up, trotted me out to the clubs, bars, parties. Though she said she cared about my career, if my work interfered with her social events, she resented it. Even tried to sabotage it by calling my supervisor and insisting I be placed on less demanding projects, and expecting to be obeyed since she was an investor. See, she believed her money and pedigree would solve any problem or situation. Including me. Because I was her toy to play with, dress up, bend and, when the time came, to put on the shelf."

"Achilles." Part of her didn't want him to finish. But again, not about her. Not about the hole he ripped in her chest with each word. So she didn't say anything else. Just continued to hold his hand.

"I finally ended it, but not because I woke up or got fed up. Only because a coworker who knew we were dating took pity on me and emailed me the engagement announcement in the Tacoma society pages. Her engagement announcement to the heir of a financial empire." His mouth twisted into a sardonic caricature of a smile. "When I confronted her about it, she waved it off. As if her upcoming marriage meant nothing. Because to her, it didn't. She expected me to remain her fucking side piece. As I'd been all along, I just hadn't known it. And she actually appeared shocked when I told her hell no. Seems no one had told her that before."

He sighed, pinched the bridge of his nose, then tunneled his fingers through his hair, dragging the strands back from his face.

"I grew up in the roughest parts of Seattle, considered myself street-smart. I'd been through—" something hard…haunted flickered in his eyes "—some shit. But the first time a beautiful woman other than my mother showed me compassion, attention, I lost myself. I became someone I didn't recognize. And I've never forgiven myself for it. I don't know if I can. Because if I do, I'll forget and I'll do it again. I can never go back to that place. Ever."

The vow came out impassioned, almost furious. But that fury was reserved for himself, the man who'd fallen for a woman who had betrayed him.

Mycah understood that kind of betrayal. The path of it might be different, but that pain? Oh, she was very familiar.

And it could break a person's spirit. Their belief and trust in other people. In themselves.

"What was her name?" she asked.

He studied her for a moment, head cocked to the side. "Yvette. Why?"

"They say if you give the devil a name and say it aloud, he—or she—no longer has power over you."

He snorted softly. "That's what they say, huh?" He shook his head, a faint smile lifting the corner of his mouth before disappearing. "Yvette." He said her name again, lower this time, and if she hadn't been so tuned in to him, she might not have caught it. He hiked his chin at her. "What's the name of your devil, Mycah?"

A spark of panic flared in her chest. Oh, God, where did she start? Easy. She didn't. Because she was afraid if she did, she wouldn't be able to stop.

"I don't have any."

"Liar," he murmured, calling her out.

His arm shot out, curling around her waist, hauling her across his thighs. He arranged her so she straddled him, and she moaned, her sex notching against his rapidly hardening cock. But before she had time to roll her hips and get ready for round—what, three or four?— he cradled her face between his hands and tipped her head down so she had no choice but to meet his unwavering scrutiny.

"You, Mycah Hill," he said, sweeping his thumb over her cheekbone, "are a liar. But that's okay. We've had enough revelations for one day. But when you're ready, I'll be here. And you're going to tell me. Because we both know you have demons. You let me know when you want to name them."

Then he took her mouth.

And took her under.

And she let him.

Ten

"I swear, one day you're going to have to explain to me why you prefer this office in the basement when there's a perfectly good one with fucking windows on the executive floor."

Achilles sighed as Cain strode into the office, scowling as he surveyed the workspace as if it were the first time he'd seen it. Which it wasn't. His older brother just never let pass an opportunity to bitch about the size and location. For some reason, it really irked Cain that Achilles preferred to be down in the IT department instead of on the thirty-second floor with Cain and Kenan.

When he asked, Achilles gave him his rote answer of feeling more comfortable with the people who "spoke his language." And it wasn't a complete lie. But neither was it the truth.

He couldn't tell Cain, or Kenan for that matter, that even something as inconsequential as taking an office next to them and appearing as a unified Farrell front constituted bonds he wasn't comfortable forming. Not when he had no intention of strengthening or tightening those bonds.

Not when he planned on returning to Washington in a matter of months.

Doing so would just make it that much harder to cut ties when the time came. And if losing his mother and Yvette's betrayal had educated him in anything, it was that love hurt.

Whether due to abandonment, lies, fists, betrayal... death.

Love always ended in pain.

No attachments. No love. No hurt.

So no, he'd keep his office here on the eighth floor and his brothers at a careful distance. It would be better for them in the long run. And definitely better for him.

"As I've repeatedly told you and Kenan, it's not the basement," he said, shifting his attention from Cain, who had dropped into the visitor's chair, and back to his monitor.

"Did I hear my name being taken in vain?" His younger brother appeared in the doorway, carefree grin in place. "Or were you saying it in total adoration? I get that a lot."

Cain snorted. "This office is already cramped. We damn sure don't have enough room in here for us and your ego."

"I told you we should've had this meeting in the

broom closet down the hall. It's more spacious." Kenan shrugged, claiming the other chair next to Cain.

"Are you two finished?" Achilles snapped. "If you feel so claustrophobic, there are perfectly good phones in your offices, and you could've used them to call me."

"What would've been the fun in that?" Kenan asked. "Besides, I love the smell of fresh asbestos in the morning."

Achilles growled, and Kenan laughed, holding up his hands, palms out.

"Fine, fine. I'm done. Cain, can we get on with this before he forgets that I'm his brother?"

As if he could. Achilles curled his fingers into his palm to prevent himself from rubbing at the pang in his chest Kenan's words generated.

"Here, Achilles." Cain leaned forward and slid a manila folder onto the desk. "I emailed you a copy of this, but here's a hard copy, too. Don't say it." He turned and jabbed a finger at Kenan, then pointed the same one at Achilles. "I know, I know. And so what? I still like to have things in my hands. Sue me."

And in the hands of others, too, but okay, he'd keep his mouth shut. That was an argument for another day.

"Anyway, we're looking at acquiring a software company out of San Francisco. Just from what we're seeing and hearing, they're really turning the software-as-a-service industry on its head with their backup technology. They're making on-premises backups obsolete with their third-party backup software app on the cloud. There haven't been security issues and it cuts costs. I'm sure there are variables we haven't uncovered, and that's where you come in. And before we invest one hundred and fifty million dollars, we need to make sure it's sound. And that we're going to make a profit, of course. Can you look it over and give us your opinion on not just the software but the company?"

Achilles blinked. Cain had requested his presence in meetings, but he'd felt like a figurehead. He hadn't offered his opinions, and he hadn't been asked for them. Here, in the IT department, he was at least useful, able to answer calls, offer help and fix problems, even install software when needed because he wasn't afraid to get his hands dirty.

But this...

He glanced away from Cain for a moment, unable to maintain eye contact with the same penetrating gaze he met in the mirror every morning. His brother, who'd suffered through too much at the abusive hands of their father, saw too much. Cain, accepted heir of Farrell and renowned businessman, wouldn't lay the fate of millions of dollars in Achilles's hands if he didn't trust him. And Achilles feared Cain would glimpse how much this show of trust, of faith, meant to him.

Because it did.

There went those bonds. Tightening. And he fought them like a man drowning, even as an image of his passion project—his video game—popped in his mind. As did the inane urge to tell his brothers about it. The longing shoved at his rib cage, growing in pressure. He needed to share it with the two people who just might be those closest to him. Who might understand him if he just opened up and let them in...

Love always ended in pain.

No attachments. No love. No hurt.

The reminder whispered through his head, echoed in his heart. And it was sharp, leaving an ache behind.

"Yes, I'll do it." Achilles picked the folder up. "When do you need the info back?"

"Next Monday work?" Cain asked.

That gave him a week, which would be more than enough time. "That's fine."

"Good." Cain stood, sliding his hands into the front pockets of his gray tailored pants. "Also, just wanted to give you a heads-up. Devon's going to be calling you. She's starting a computer class at the community center since a new donor anonymously donated PCs."

Kenan coughed.

"Shut up, you," Cain snapped. "Anyway, I didn't want you to be ambushed." He paused. "But you should know, my fiancée has a soft heart. And even if you decide to tell her no, let her down gently or I'll steal those Dr. Who collectibles in your desk drawer that you think we don't know about and sell them online for a penny."

Achilles gaped at Cain, caught between shock and laughter.

"I think you broke him," Kenan whispered.

More of those bonds.

"Okay, got it," Achilles rasped.

Moments later, his brothers left, and Achilles still stared at the door. Finally, shaking his head, he got back to work. And if his chest felt a little lighter, well, he attributed it to the challenge of a new project, nothing else.

Hours later, a knock at his office door brought his head up, and another kind of warmth streamed through him. Molten. Greedy. Which made sense, since Mycah stood in his doorway. It'd been a couple of days since he'd seen her, sharpening the need inside him to a knife's edge.

He glanced at the clock at the bottom of his computer monitor. Several minutes after seven. That meant they were most likely the only ones left on his floor. He rose from his chair as she stepped inside, closing the door behind her.

It'd been almost two months since that night at her parents' disastrous dinner party—since they'd had sex on his living room floor. And on his couch. And in his bed.

Not that it'd been the last night they'd spent together. More had followed. Many more. But by tacit agreement, they'd kept it between them, a secret, not allowing what they did to each other after hours to cross the boundaries into the office. Since they rarely saw one another, no issues had arisen. Still, he was cognizant that he was an owner of the company…at least for the next several months. And because she'd made her worries about her professional reputation very clear, he ensured he didn't cause any tongues to wag by behavior on his part.

Still… He would be lying if he didn't admit that the secrecy irritated him like a pebble in an ill-fitting shoe. After Yvette, he'd vowed never to be someone's dirty little secret. Never to allow anyone to make him feel as if he were unworthy. And while he understood Mycah's very valid concerns for her career, he couldn't help the seeds of doubt that had never been fully up-rooted; they'd been sown in hurt and betrayal. The similarities between then and now crept into his mind after the passion cooled and she curled next to him or left his apartment.

Coming to him in the cover of darkness.

Pretending they weren't lovers around others of influence.

Conscripting him to live a lie.

But then she'd touch him. And the need trumped what he'd ever experienced with any other woman, even Yvette. The loneliness that he'd convinced himself didn't bother him disappeared.

Maybe he was worrying over nothing, though. Unlike with Yvette, he recognized this...arrangement with Mycah couldn't go anywhere. It had an expiration date and a definite conclusion. For both of them.

"Hey," he said, rounding the desk. "What're you doing here? I thought we were meeting at the— What's wrong?"

He pulled up short, for the first time noticing the stark look in her eyes and the tension holding her body unnaturally rigid.

She parted her lips, and they moved but no sound emerged. Unease pulsed through him, and he stepped toward her, but she shook her head, holding up a hand, and he stopped. Though everything in him demanded he go to her, pull her to him, slay and then fix whatever it was that had darkened her gaze to nearly black.

"I'm pregnant."

Eleven

I'm pregnant.

Her announcement reverberated in the room like a shout. Except instead of gradually quieting, it seemed to gain volume, growing louder and louder until it assaulted her ears, boomed in her head. Of course, that was her imagination, but staring into Achilles's stern face, the honed slashes of his cheekbones and jaw jutting out in stark relief under his taut, golden-brown skin... Well, she could be forgiven for her dark flight of fancy.

Not that she could blame him.

She'd had two days to absorb the fact that she—a twenty-nine-year-old professional woman well versed in the mechanics of sex—had fucked up and ended up pregnant. Yes, *she*. Because ultimately this was *her* body, *her* responsibility. No one would love it, care for it, protect it like she could—was supposed to. No, it wasn't all on her, because hell, he'd been there. But she'd known she hadn't been on any other contraception; there hadn't been any need since she... She squeezed her eyes shut. Damn that heat of the moment and that one and only time that had seemed so harmless... Turned out, it hadn't been.

Fear slicked a path through the highway of her veins, leaving dangerous black ice behind. Oh, God, she was scared. So fucking scared. And alone. For two days, she'd called in sick, claiming a stomach flu when in truth, she'd lain curled up in bed, shell-shocked, grappling with her new reality. A new reality that had twisted and warped into this alternate universe with a plus sign on a stick.

Her job. Her lifestyle. Her family. Those had been her first thoughts, as selfish as they'd been. And she could admit that they had been selfish. She'd worked hard for years to get where she was now. This was just the beginning. There were so many more years of work to put in, and regardless of the foolish woman she'd been years earlier, she hadn't imagined a man and baby in her life now. Some women wanted all of that and managed it beautifully—she wasn't one of them. Besides, she enjoyed the freedom of being single, of not having to answer to anyone. Of doing something as simple as going out to dinner or to the store when she wanted— by herself. Or going on vacation. She'd heard enough from friends with kids to know she could kiss that carefree lifestyle goodbye.

And then her family. Jesus. A child out of wedlock. They'd disown her. Even discovering the identity of the father wouldn't appease them. Finding out Achilles was the father might be worse because he was the bastard, the thug, in their eyes. The nobody. Anger rushed through her. Not that they knew what they were talking about since they'd never even given him a chance.

As suddenly as the anger entered, the emotion evaporated like smoke, leaving her exhausted.

None of those reasons that had bombarded her mattered in the end, though.

Because as she'd stared at another dawn creeping over the horizon, chasing away the night, a certain bone-deep knowledge drove away her doubts.

She was keeping the baby.

Her baby.

Along with that knowledge had come a love so simple, yet so profound. And now, standing in front of Achilles, that love for something—someone, because it was already someone to her—the size of a bean had already consumed her whole.

"You're pregnant."

He stated it rather than asked, but she nodded anyway, instinctively crossing her arms low over her stomach where their child slept. Of course that perceptive but inscrutable gaze didn't miss the gesture, and his gaze dropped to her belly, remaining there for several long moments before returning to her face.

"What're your plans?" he asked, voice even, calm. Too calm.

His guarded expression, careful tone… They revealed nothing of his thoughts, and she couldn't gauge him. It was the Achilles from the bar, and her heart thudded against her sternum. *What do you want?* her mind railed. *Tell me if you want this baby.*

But she didn't loose those words. Didn't go to him, pound her fists against that brick wall of a chest and act a fool. Maybe he had the right of it. Emotions didn't belong here between them. After all, hadn't messy *emotions* gotten her here in the first place?

If she'd spent only that one night with him like she'd promised herself instead of... *Say it,* her ruthless mind insisted. If she'd stuck to the one-night rule instead of giving in to how he made her feel, they wouldn't be in this situation. Not just the physical pleasure. As amazing as that was, the hedonism of stripping free of the "Hill" layers and just being Mycah, just being herself, had proved far more addictive. She hadn't been ready to give that up.

And now they both had to pay the cost. Or at least she did. And she would, willingly and gladly.

Notching her chin high, she straightened her shoulders and met that cold, lupine stare.

"I'm keeping it." Her arms tightened around her middle. "I'm keeping the baby."

Fire blazed in his gaze, melting the ice. "Good."

"Good?" she whispered, shock whipping through her. She hadn't been expecting that. Or the... Wait... "You're happy about this?"

For the first time since she'd dropped the bombshell, he betrayed a reaction. Well, no, that wasn't exactly true. There'd been that breath-stealing flicker of heat in his eyes. But he dragged a hand through his hair, dislodging the tie at the back of his head. He removed it, tossing the band on the desk behind him, and didn't immediately turn back around. Instead, he braced his hands on the desktop, his broad back straining against the material of his white shirt.

Finally, he pivoted, and the shadows in his eyes... Her chest seized, an invisible clamp reaching inside and squeezing her ribs so she could barely breathe.

"Happy. I think that's too easy." His fingers flexed next to his thighs before he seemed to catch the movement and deliberately stilled it. "You know who my father is—a man who impregnated my mother, then abandoned her. Threw her away like she—like we— were trash. But the men who followed? Barron was the kindest."

That clamp around her sternum clinched tighter and tighter. And she ground her teeth together to imprison the whimper that clawed at the back of her throat. She didn't think Achilles would appreciate the sympathy it conveyed. He'd probably mistake it for pity when it wasn't. There was absolutely nothing to pity about this man.

"I didn't have a good male role model. Most of the boys I knew growing up didn't, either. I had my mother and grandmother, but they couldn't teach me about fatherhood. What I learned about manhood, I got from the men my mom brought around. And they taught me what I didn't want to be, what not to do. How not to treat a woman and a child. But was it enough? I don't know." He shook his head, spread his hands wide, studying the big palms as if they contained the answers that hadn't been passed down to him growing up. After a moment, he lifted his head, looked at her. "So am I happy? Yes. Maybe. But more than that I'm terrified I'll fuck up."

"You've met my parents, right?" Mycah murmured. When Achilles blinked, then snorted, she softly laughed. "I've had two days to process this. And I'm scared, too. I grew up with two parents in a wealthy home, affluent neighborhood, great schools, with every privilege and opportunity afforded me. And yet, I'm what some might call emotionally stunted, care too much what others think, seek validation in my career and am terrified of my parents' rejection even knowing they are elitists, classists and just damn mean. So I have baggage, too, and yes, am equally terrified of fucking up. But maybe that's what will make us good parents. If we believed we were going to be perfect, we would be setting ourselves up for failure. If we go into this knowing we're going to make mistakes, that we're far from perfect, then we'll be vigilant, careful and, most of all, we'll be forgiving. Of ourselves and our child."

He exhaled a breath. Nodded. "Okay, that makes sense." He paused. Nodded again. "Thank you." Clearing his throat, he stretched an arm toward her, then dropped it. Frowning, he asked, "Where do we go from here? Have you seen a doctor?"

"I set up an appointment for tomorrow morning. I—" She crossed her arms over her chest, rubbing her hands up and down as if she could warm herself. Impossible when the cold emanated from within. "I don't want to exclude you from the pregnancy, I promise you I don't.

But you might not be able to go to my doctor appointment with me tomorrow."

His frown deepened, lightning flashing in his eyes. "Why?"

"Because I share the same ob-gyn as my mother, and while doctor-patient confidentiality is supposed to be sacred, I don't want to risk it. So I'm going to confirm the pregnancy tomorrow. I'll find another doctor's office so we can both attend the appointments."

Slowly, his expression cleared, but shadows remained in his gaze. Still, he nodded. "Fine."

"Also," she continued, blowing out a puff of air. "If you don't mind, I want to keep the pregnancy a secret for now. At least for the first trimester. You might not understand—"

He leaned back against his desk, curling his fingers around the edge. "Then make me."

Thrusting her hands through her curls, she paced away several steps, gathering her chaotic thoughts. How to make him see without once again making this about her? But in a way, it *was* about her. Because as Barron had shown with his mother, at any point, Achilles could walk away, and she would be left alone, her life irrevocably changed.

She drew to a halt several feet in front of him.

"Call me superstitious but the first trimester is the most fragile time of a pregnancy, where miscarriages can occur. And I'd rather wait until we're free of it and in the second trimester before telling anyone. Second, I just started this job at Farrell. I need to figure out how to tell your brothers that not only am I pregnant but by their brother, co-CEO of the company—a man I pretended not to know during my job interview. And then deal with how that will appear to the employees and the business community as a whole, and how it will affect my reputation. Third, I have to decide how I'm going to tell my parents. And prepare myself for that fallout. So yes, I'm asking you for time."

He silently studied her, and finally he pushed himself off the desk and strode the short steps toward her, eliminating the small space separating them. His chest brushed against hers, his thighs grazing hers. Despite the situation, his scent, the firm pressure of his big body touching hers, lit her up.

"It really sucks that you got knocked up by the Feral Farrell, doesn't it?" he asked softly. Almost gently. Which made the question even more blasphemous.

"Don't you say that," she said, her voice vehement, furious. "Don't you ever fucking say that again."

He arched a dark brow, his bright gaze impenetrable once more. "Don't worry. I won't say a word. Now, is that it? Any more conditions?"

She shook her head. "Achilles—"

"Good. Call me after the appointment and let me know what the doctor said."

He turned away from her and stalked across the office, returning to his desk. Dismissing her. The punch of pain to her chest shouldn't have surprised her; she wasn't a stranger to it. Yet it still drove the air from her lungs.

But damn if she'd let him know it.

She'd promised herself long ago that she'd never

allow herself to become emotionally entangled again. To never give anyone else the opportunity to reject her. She'd failed herself on both accounts.

She wouldn't do it again.

Not when she now had too much to lose.

Twelve

I'm on my way over. I need to talk to you. It's important.

Mycah stared at the text and debated pretending that she didn't see it. No, that wouldn't work. Her mother would see that she'd read it.

She glanced down at her long-sleeved white shirt, black lounge pants and bare feet. If she shoved on sneakers quickly, threw on a coat and grabbed her car keys, she might be able to make it out of the house before her mother made it over here.

The doorbell rang, dispelling that hope.

Shit.

Mycah clapped a hand to her forehead.

Why? Why had she bought a condo in the same neighborhood as her parents' home? She should've taken that cute apartment in Charlestown like she'd wanted. Right. Because of Angelique. When she was her sister's age, she'd wished for a place to escape to when her parents had become too overbearing. Mycah had wanted to give that haven to her sister. Too bad Laurence and Cherise knew the location, as well.

Sighing, Mycah headed across her hardwood floor toward the front door, the exhaustion that had sent her home from work early suddenly feeling heavier.

Her first doctor's appointment had been earlier in the week, and it seemed like as soon as she'd officially confirmed the pregnancy, all the symptoms she'd ever heard and read about—morning sickness, fatigue, breast and abdomen soreness—had visited upon her like plagues. Achilles had been supportive: asking questions about the appointment, inquiring about her health, even picking up her neonatal vitamins after work when she'd been too tired to do anything but go home.

But one thing he hadn't done—*they* hadn't done—was resume their former relationship. If their secret, no-strings, sexual arrangement could be called that. Whatever it'd been, it was over. He hadn't tried to touch her, hadn't asked to spend the night, hadn't asked her to come over to the penthouse.

She should be grateful.

Because any kind of attachment other than co-parenting wouldn't be wise.

And they hadn't even had a chance to discuss the mechanics of that yet. How he planned to co-parent from across the country. Literally.

Until I'm free from it all.

His words continued to haunt her, even months later. He was leaving. She couldn't forget that.

Couldn't forget the reality of it. What it meant not just for her, but for their baby.

Before... Before a plus sign turned up on a stick, flipping her world on its head, she'd been in danger of forgetting that the "just sex" relationship she and Achilles had didn't have a fairy-tale ending. Even then, the odds had been stacked so high against them that she would've needed an Atlas-sized ladder to see over them.

Achilles's resenting anything or anyone having to do with the wealthy world she came from. Their employer/employee relationship. The potential damage to her professional reputation if their intimate relationship ever got out.

Still... She'd forgotten the main issue that trumped everything else.

There'd been no "them."

Because Achilles had never intended on staying in Boston. His home was back in Washington, where he belonged.

And if she were honest with herself, could she give up her career, give up this part of herself for him? She'd been ready to do that for a man before. To place his happiness, his career, above her own. She'd loved him so much that she'd willingly turned a blind eye to his character, even when he'd shown her who he was. And when he'd stolen her proposal for a new diversity, equity and inclusion program, submitted it as his own and ended up receiving a promotion for it? She'd been devastated, damn near destroyed by the betrayal.

That heartbreak had taught her that men, parents, colleagues could disappoint and even crush her. But only she could control if she allowed it. Only she could control herself.

They couldn't hurt her if she didn't permit them access to the core of her. At some point in her life, she'd let each of them have that access, and they'd betrayed her. Almost destroyed her. Used her.

Never again.

Achilles hadn't committed any of those sins yet.

Yet.

But he more than any of those in her past had the power to wreak the worst damage—a damage she might not be able to recover from.

So yes, she was grateful they hadn't resumed that part of their relationship.

It was for the best.

No physical entanglements meant she didn't open herself to messy emotional ones. If she didn't protect herself, no one else would. God knows, history had proved that one out.

And if she didn't protect herself, then how could she be there for her baby?

The doorbell rang again, more insistent this time.

No more putting off this visit. Hell, the sooner she got it done, the quicker it would be over with and she could return to bed.

She paused to glance through the peephole—this was Back Bay but still not immune to crime and she was no fool—then unlocked the door and opened it to her mother.

"Mom."

"Hello, honey." Cherise swept inside, her light floral scent swamping Mycah as she brushed kisses over both her cheeks. "I'm glad you were home. You claim to be so busy lately. Too busy for your parents."

Guilt Trip 501. Graduate level.

"Your text said you needed to see me about something important." Mycah shut the door and moved toward the living room. Her mother frowned in disapproval as Mycah sank to the couch cushions, but God, she was *tired*. And call it sixth sense, but something told her she needed to sit down for the bullshit that was headed her way.

"It is important, honey." Lowering to the armchair across from the couch, Cherise perched on the edge, perfect and immaculate in an elegant, dark green pantsuit even at six o'clock in the evening. "Margaret Dansing mentioned she saw you and Cain Farrell downtown having lunch last week."

Mycah arched a brow, irritation sparking inside her. "The eagle-eyed Mrs. Dansing would be correct. It was a business lunch. That's the important issue?"

"No, I just thought it was interesting. She commented on what a striking couple you made. I have to admit, I agreed." Cherise toyed with an earring, but Mycah wasn't fooled by the casual gesture or tone.

"Mother, please tell me you shut that gossip down. For the millionth time, Cain is just my employer. If Margaret Dansing had stuck around a little bit longer, she would've seen a couple more people from my department join us. And for the millionth and one time, Cain has a fiancée. One he looks even more striking with."

Her mother waved a hand. "Engagements end all the time. All I'm saying is you need to keep your options open."

"Mother," Mycah ground out between gritted teeth. "What was so important?"

Cherise sighed. "Fine. Mycah, your father and I are worried about you."

Out of respect, Mycah managed not to roll her eyes. Barely. This "we're worried about you" speech came about once a quarter. It was a little early, but not unexpected.

"I'm fine, Mom. Now, if that's all—"

"Mycah, first this insistence of working at all these jobs—"

"Two, Mom. I've worked at two. One for seven years."

"It would be one thing if you at least worked for Hill-Harper."

Mycah snorted at that. No way in hell. And be under not just her father's thumb but at the mercy of a board of people who remembered her when she was in Pull-Ups? Zero chance of respect.

"Then you bring home that…that man to dinner," her mother sneered.

"If memory serves me correctly, and it does, you invited him to dinner, and you did it to be spiteful. Just to humiliate him for the entertainment of your guests." Fury rose inside Mycah as she uncurled her legs from under her, leaning forward and pinning her mother with a glare. "You and Dad are just angry because he turned the tables and threw your snobbery back in your faces and embarrassed you in front of your guests."

"As if he could." Her mother sniffed, picking non-existent lint off her pants. "He just exhibited his poor breeding and manners."

"I'm sure that's what he said about you two."

"Mycah Hill," Cherise snapped. "Don't you dare talk to me like that. I'm your mother and you'll show me respect."

"Believe me, Mom. I am." She blew out a breath and shook her head. "You and Dad disappointed me that night. Why do you think I haven't been back since then?"

"Well, the feeling is entirely mutual," her mother said, voice as cold as the winter wind. "Taking his side over your family. Chasing after him. You barely know that thug and we're your family."

"You don't know him, either, and don't call him another name in my house or in front of me."

Her mother's chin snapped back a little at Mycah's equally cool tone, then her eyes narrowed, mouth thinning.

"Well, is that how it is?" She tilted her head to the side, studying Mycah. "Are you involved with this… man? Is that why you've appointed yourself his zealous defender?"

"No, we aren't involved." *Anymore. But he's the father of your grandchild.* God, how she longed to say it. But by sheer will she bit back the words. "But he doesn't deserve your antipathy. You've made him a target because of who his mother is and where he's from and what he wasn't born with. When, if circumstances were different, given the color of your skin and the country you live in, you stripped away your money and fancy address, some of the people you call friends would talk to you in the same way."

Face tight, Cherise rose from the chair, anger vibrating off her stiff form.

"Your father and I have only wanted what's best for you. We've tried to guide you in the right direction, yet you've rebelled, slapped our hands, scorned our efforts at every turn. Have you ever looked down from your high horse to wonder how that made us feel? You're ungrateful. Excuse us for loving you."

With the regality of a queen, she swept from the room and out of the apartment, the door closing softly behind her. Because even in her anger, her mother would never slam a door.

Mycah stared at the empty living room entrance, numb.

You're ungrateful. Excuse us for loving you.
You're ungrateful. Excuse us for loving you.

The accusations played over and over in her head like a scratch-free, newly minted record. And each time they rebounded off the walls of her mind, the ice in her body spread a little further, capturing another part of her in the emotional frostbite.

Good. Because she didn't want to feel.

"Mycah?" A hand cupped her cheek, and she jerked from it, the warmth of that palm almost too much for the cold. She needed the cold. "Mycah?" Another hand cradled the other side of her face, forcing her to focus, to look at the person who refused to leave her in the comforting cold. "Baby, look at me. What's wrong?"

With no choice, she looked. Focused. And met an all-too-familiar sight. Achilles's frown. "Achilles?" she murmured. "What are you doing here?"

"I knocked but you didn't answer. And the door was unlocked." Reproach colored his tone but, again, she was too numb to take offense. His thumbs caressed her cheekbones. "I called your name, but you didn't answer. What's wrong? You seem…off."

Nothing.

It sat on her tongue, because God. She was so damn tired of explaining. Of saying the wrong things that set people off and hurt them. "Nothing" seemed the safest, but when she parted her lips…

"She called me ungrateful. And maybe I am. I've said that about myself often enough. I'm selfish, too. Look at what I've done with you. Used you for your body, even though you did some using, too. But we both got orgasms out of it, so I think the exchange rate was pretty fair there. But ungrateful with them? How? Tell me how. By trying to be the perfect daughter even when I wanted to run away to a circus. A literal fucking circus. I was ten, on a class trip, and I snuck behind the tent and was five minutes from sneaking into a clown's trunk. Only fear of being the circus's tigers' next meal made me go back and find my class."

Achilles choked. "Mycah—"

She gripped his thick wrists, clinging to them as if his solid body were the only thing anchoring her to the earth. "No, I'm serious. By getting straight As and graduating top of my class and going to the best college? Supporting them for years with the job they scorned? I'm not worthy because I don't have a billionaire husband and head several charity committees and host social events of the year? My ring finger, vagina and womb are more important than my brain. Yet, without me, they would be out on the street. But *I'm ungrateful.* They destroy me with their criticism. Their dismissal of my successes. Their derision of my perceived lack of femininity. Meanwhile, sometimes, I think I'm strangling from the responsibility of carrying this family and their expectations. And yet I do it. You asked me why I do it. Do you remember that?"

"Yes, baby, I remember," he whispered.

"Because I want their love. I want them to accept me for who I am, to love me for me. But that means sacrificing my own dreams, my own desires, and conforming to theirs. Just like they're already starting to do with Angelique. She said to excuse her for loving me. I can't." Mycah tightened her grip on him, tugging, closing her eyes. "I can't excuse her. Because their love comes at too high a price. My identity. My peace. My…soul."

When the last word left her, she wilted, as if the outpouring sapped the last of her strength. Achilles caught her, hauling her against his chest. He rose, holding her in his arms as if she weighed nothing, and took her place on the couch. And when the numbness cracked down the middle, and the hurt, anger and sorrow gushed in, drowning her, she didn't fight it.

She sobbed her disappointment, her outrage, her

pain, her fear. How long she curled on his lap, pressed against his chest, she didn't know. But by the time she glanced up, the sky outside the bay windows had deepened from purple to black, casting dark shadows across Achilles's face.

A chasm of emptiness yawned wide in her chest, but unlike the numbing from earlier, this was...cleansing. Sighing, she shifted, wincing at the weariness that weighed down her limbs. She should get up, move, say something. At least apologize to Achilles for losing her shit, then crying all over him.

Before she had a chance to decide which one to do first, he stood, still holding her in his arms. She gasped, wrapping her arms around his neck, and even that effort was almost beyond her at the moment.

"Bedroom?" he asked.

"Down the hall. Last room on the right."

He didn't speak again, just followed her instructions. In moments, he entered her room. Not bothering to turn on the lights, he set her on the bed and left, making his way to the en suite bathroom.

The light flicked on, and seconds later, the sound of running water reached her. Surprise whispered through her, but she didn't have time to dwell on it because he returned, gently grasping her waist and bringing her back to her feet. With a quick efficiency that didn't contain sensuality but only tenderness, he removed her clothes and once more lifted her against his chest.

No words were spoken as he settled her in the warm bath, removed the tie from his own hair, gathered her curls on top of her head and bathed her. In other circumstances, she would've objected. She'd always been the caretaker, the provider, the one in control. But now, as Achilles smoothed the bath cloth over her shoulders, arms and breasts, she handed that control over to him. Let him care for her. Wash her. Pick her up out of the tub and pat her dry.

When he carried her back to her bedroom, slipped her between the sheets and climbed in behind her, she didn't protest. No, she welcomed his hard, protective body curled around her. This wasn't about sex. It wasn't about expectation.

And as she drifted to sleep, for the first time in longer than she could remember, peace filled her.

Thirteen

Achilles raised his arms above his head, stretching them toward the beautiful, vaulted ceiling of Mycah's living room. Groaning at the burn in his muscles, he lowered his arms, exhaling and surveying the room he'd temporarily commandeered as his workspace.

As soon as Mycah had fallen into a deep sleep, he'd slid out of bed, retrieved his laptop bag from his car and set up just down the hall so if she needed him, he could hear her. After that meltdown, no way in hell he was leaving her alone tonight. She shouldn't be alone. He had the feeling she was alone too often.

And yeah, he definitely caught the pot-calling-the-kettle-black hypocrisy of that.

Leaning back against the couch cushion, he took in the surprisingly warm, cozy apartment. If a person could call huge bay windows with ornate designs, a massive fireplace that nearly spanned one wall, beautiful hardwood walls, floor-to-ceiling fully packed bookshelves and gorgeous molding something as simple as an apartment. Still, he liked it much better than the penthouse where he stayed. Here, trees filled her view, and in her spacious bedroom with its exposed brick walls, he'd snagged a glimpse of a garden outside her window. Even her kitchen looked like an actual kitchen—homey, lived in, with a table, chairs, wood cabinets, windows—instead of something out of a futuristic sci-fi movie.

Mycah had even decorated it with furniture meant for comfort instead of appearance. The overstuffed couches and chairs, earth tones and jeweled pillows, throw rugs, standing lamps, Afrocentric art—they all invited a person to sit down, curl their feet underneath themselves, talk, stay. A far cry from her parents' house that screamed "this is staged so you know how affluent, powerful and important we are."

The apartment wasn't the only surprising aspect he'd learned about Mycah.

Jesus.

Her pain.

So much of it, she'd cracked under the weight.

He propped his elbows on his thighs, digging his thumbs into his eyes, rubbing them. How could her parents not look at her and be proud of the woman she was? Not appreciate all that she sacrificed for them? Despite how they chose to show it, he didn't doubt that Laurence and Cherise loved Mycah. But that love came with conditions. And those conditions were asphyxiating the relationship with their daughter as surely as weeds choking the life from flowers straining to reach the sun.

A muted sound came from the direction of Mycah's bedroom, and he tilted his head toward it, frowning, listening. Several seconds passed, and just as his muscles loosened and he returned to his laptop to resume working, the sound reached him again. He recognized it.

Surging from the couch, he strode down the corridor, entered Mycah's bedroom and headed for the bathroom. He spotted her, hunched over the toilet and clinging to it as she vomited into the porcelain bowl.

Kneeling next to her, he murmured her name, rubbing soothing circles on her back, feeling...helpless. Not an easy thing for a man to admit. As soon as she'd told him about the pregnancy, he'd read everything he could about it—especially that first trimester. So he knew morning sickness—a misnomer if he ever heard one—was normal for most women, but he hated to see her suffer like this and not be able to do anything to help her. He'd witnessed his fair share of people puking. Some of the men his mother had dated. In high school. In jail. College. But this was different. With them, he hadn't wished he could trade places, take their misery on for himself.

Standing, he moved across the large bathroom, grabbed a bath cloth from the linen closet and wet it under the faucet. He folded it a couple of times and returned to her, settling it on the back of her neck as his mother had done for him when he'd been sick.

"You don't have to—" Another bout of retching cut her off, her back bowing under the force of it. She moaned as the last of it passed, a tremor shaking her.

"Yes, I do." He shifted behind her, curving his body around hers, lending her his strength, even though, realistically, it was an impossibility. Still, she could lean on him. Know he was there for her. He kissed the top of her curls. "I'm not leaving, baby, so don't ask."

Another groan. "I don't want you to see me like this."

He scoffed. "I've seen those birthing videos. In seven months, I'm going to see you looking a hell of a lot worse. This is nothing."

She reached behind her and weakly slapped him. "That's a really messed-up thing to say. And don't remind— Oh, God."

For the next ten minutes they remained in the bathroom, and when they finally emerged, with her tired and clothed in fresh pajamas, Achilles led her to the living room and tucked her in on the couch. He rummaged in her kitchen, and soon returned to her with a steaming cup of peppermint tea and a slice of toast.

"It's not much," he said, sitting both the cup and the small plate on the table in front of her. "But it'll settle your stomach. And from what I've read, both are good to help ease the morning sickness."

"Thank you," she murmured, reaching for the tea and sipping from the cup. "That doesn't surprise me."

"What?" He lowered to the couch next to her, shifting his laptop, bag and manuals over to give her room.

"That you've been reading up on it. Watching videos." She studied him over the rim of the cup. "I don't think I've met anyone with a hungrier brain than yours."

"That sounds…disturbing."

The corner of her mouth quirked in a sardonic half smile. "It's a compliment. You're voracious for information. It's what makes you so brilliant. And so intimidating, too. People look at the hair, the ink, the size—" she waved a hand up and down in front of him "—and underestimate you. For instance, my parents' party. I didn't even know that about my ancestors. Not that I'm ashamed of it. I think it's cool as hell. Still, I didn't know. But you did. Like I said. Information. And you wielded it like a double-edged sword."

"Unexpected?" He heard the edge in his voice, wished he could dull it. But years of being on the "You're smart for being poor/brown/an ex-con" end of the stick was hard to shake.

"For them maybe," she admitted softly. "But not for me."

Silence thrummed in the room, and they stared at each other, a tension thick with words unspoken, desire a living, breathing entity right there with them.

"Eat," he finally said, nodding toward the plate and the untouched toast. "You need to coat your stomach."

"More things you read?" she teased, that faint smile touching her sensual mouth. But she did pick up the bread and nibble on it. "What are you working on so late?" she asked, dipping her head toward his laptop. "Is there a project from the office that you had to bring home?"

Achilles shifted his attention to his computer. He

stood on a precipice, one of trust. No one knew about the video game. Not even Cain and Kenan. He glanced at Mycah, who slowly frowned the longer he remained quiet. His heart thudded, echoing in his head until all he heard was its bass rhythm. His tongue thickened, nerves twisting in his gut like a nest of snakes.

This was important because *she* was important. As much as he wanted to deny it, Mycah had crawled beneath his skin, into his bones, into his soul. She wielded the power to hurt him like no other, not even his brothers. And exposing this vulnerable part of himself to her—this project that encapsulated his passion, his hopes, his dreams—meant taking a leap of faith in her.

In the faith that she wouldn't reject the truth of him.

He touched the mouse, bringing the screen to life, and with a few more taps, opened the file with the video game art. For several moments, he studied the digital image of a ravaged land, a castle in the distance, a forest with malevolent blinking red eyes glaring from its depths, and in the foreground, a lone Black teenager, his locs falling around his face, in a white T-shirt and light blue jeans and a long, gleaming sword in hand. Inhaling a deep breath, he turned the laptop toward her. She scanned the monitor, then shifted wide eyes back to him.

"What is this?" she breathed.

"Mine." And again, hearing the defensiveness in his tone, he tried again. "A video game I've been working on for the past year. It's a high-fantasy, open-world, action-adventure video game."

She huffed out a soft laugh, returning her gaze to

the laptop. "I have no idea what that means. Except for high fantasy. But the rest of that? I'm lost."

"Open world is where players can explore the game and choose for themselves how to approach the world and its particular challenges. Action-adventure games combine the best elements of both kinds of games. Just-adventure games have situation problems for players to resolve but little to no action. And action games center on real-time interactions between players that test their reflexes. Action-adventure games combine both—problem-solving and testing the reflexes."

"Angelique would be crushing so hard on you right now." Mycah flashed him a smile. "I really need to introduce you to her."

A banner of warmth unfurled inside him, even though a voice cautioned him that it was probably a throwaway comment on her part. To introduce him to her sister meant telling her parents about the baby and his being the father.

And she's too ashamed of you to do that.

Right. She needed time to prepare herself and them. Months.

The reminder doused that flare of warmth.

"Why this world?" she asked, her finger circling over the screen. "Why did you choose this particular setting?"

He hesitated, but said, "I'm not sure what you know about my past…"

"Only what the media has reported."

"I grew up in a rough neighborhood of Seattle called White Center. Back then crime, gangs and drugs had a grip on the area. Mom worked most nights, and by the time I was eleven, my grandmother had died, and I stayed in our apartment by myself. It wasn't anything to hear drug deals, fighting or gunfire in the alley behind our building. I was so immune to it, I'd just turn up the TV to drown it out. There wasn't any calling the cops."

The memories worked themselves back in, vines sprouting from seeds he'd thought long dormant. The fear of being home alone, wishing his mother was with him. Missing his grandmother.

"Still, with all that around me, my mother made sure I never got caught up in drugs or gangs. Even though she came in dragging, dog-tired and bleary-eyed at five o'clock in the morning after a night shift, she got me up, made my lunch, walked me to the bus stop, met me there after school, helped me with my homework, fixed dinner and then went to work. When she noticed I had an aptitude for computers, she took on more shifts and found a way to enroll me in college-level computer courses because I wasn't being challenged enough in high school. She always made a way. I graduated high school in the top ten percent of my class because of her. I was accepted to college because of her... And then I failed her by going to jail."

He remained silent, watching the shock wash over Mycah's face. Waited for the disgust or at least the unease as she realized she was in a room—that she'd gotten pregnant by—the thug her parents, the media called him.

But the disgust never came.

Compassion did.

And he had to battle past his first instinctive defense—slam up his guard. Reject what he perceived as pity.

Then she touched him. Covered his clenched hand with her smaller, more delicate one, and his walls cracked and tumbled down.

"Tell me," she said, her thumb brushing over his knuckles.

And he did. The story he'd never shared with anyone pouring out of him as she held his hand, his gaze and his heart.

"My mom... Like, I said, she gave me everything, all of her. So I never begrudged her the little bit of life she grabbed for herself, even if the men she chose were... lacking. It's like she had a radar for unemployed, drunk users. Most of them were jerks but harmless, but the last one..."

A fine tension invaded his body as he traveled back to that night ten years ago in their White Center apartment. His mother and her boyfriend arriving home after a night out at the local bar. Both had been drinking. Arguing. Getting louder and louder.

"Achilles, look at me." A hand cupped his cheek and he opened his eyes. He hadn't realized he'd closed them. "Keep those beautiful eyes on me. Go ahead. Finish it."

He nodded, squeezed her hand and drew it down to his thigh.

"One night, Mom came home from a date with her new boyfriend. Matt." His mouth twisted around the name, a thin layer of grime covering his tongue. "They'd been dating for two weeks and he was different from the others. There was nothing harmless about him.

He had an edge to him. Mean. Hard…" Achilles shook his head. "They were a little drunk and were arguing. I was in my room and tried to ignore it. She wouldn't have appreciated me interfering, anyway. But then I heard her cry out in pain. I bolted out of my bedroom into the living room and he had her on the floor, hitting her. I…I snapped. I punched him. And I kept punching him. I found out later that the neighbors overheard and called the cops. Next thing I know, I was in cuffs and hauled off to jail."

He slid his hand out from under hers. He spread both of his hands out and stared at his fingers as if he could still see the bruised and swollen knuckles stained with Matt's blood. Could still feel the pain from beating a man unconscious.

It didn't take much to conjure the horror that had filled him at his actions.

"I ended up serving two years for the assault. Only my mother's testimony, my clean record and Matt's not-so-clean record kept me from more time. But while I was in, I saw men—boys, really—just like me who'd made mistakes. One bad decision that had led them there. Whether it was made in the heat of the moment or done years ago and set them on a path of more poor decisions. Yes, some of them belonged right where they were, there's no denying that. But others? Others didn't have the ability to see anything different. And when I was locked up in that cell, I started dreaming about this game. And the idea stayed with me after I graduated college after I was released from jail, and years later after I started working with the software design company. What story could I tell? But more importantly, for youth like me, like the men I was locked up with, like the girls I went to school with who were told they were worth no more than their bodies and smile… What could I get them to see?"

He grabbed his laptop, clicked a few keys and pulled up more game art. This one depicted the same teen stepping through a portal. One side was the world from the previous art and on the other side was a present-day urban inner city. A kid from one world stepping into an unknown one.

"You asked why the high-fantasy setting?" Achilles asked Mycah. "Think about every movie or book you've seen or read from that genre, set in that world. When you meet the characters, they don't know their purpose yet. The most important thing for all of us is finding our identity, our reason for being. Because when we do, we begin to understand why we're here. We begin to have hope."

He shook his head. "I'm not saying this game will give kids those answers, but I am saying research has proven that video games stimulate the brain. Can actually change it in some regions. So instead of giving them a game that aggrandizes what they see every day—crime, violence, debasement of their community and people—what about a game that will awaken their brains to more? Create a different mindset and passion for something that elevates them above the reality they already know? Spark a vision in them where they see themselves as heroes, warriors, kings, queens, where they make connections and fight as a team for a common goal instead of against one another? I want to create a game where they can escape the horrors of their current environment long enough to glimpse something different, something greater. To connect with it. To see they have potential and purpose."

As the last word echoed between them, he braced himself against the regret that tried to creep in. From the vulnerability of exposing that part of himself.

"I'm so damn awed by you," Mycah rasped. She sucked in an audible breath and leaned back, pressing the heels of her palms to her eyes. "Give me a minute. It's the freaking pregnancy hormones."

Huffing out a short laugh, Achilles cuffed her wrists and gently drew her arms down. She kept her eyes squeezed closed, but after a moment she opened them, and her dark gaze glistened.

"I'm serious." She rose on her knees, tunneled her fingers through his hair, fisting the strands and tipping her head forward until it pressed to his. "What was your mother's name?"

"Natia Lee."

"Natia Lee," she breathed. "Without even meeting her, I know she was very proud of the boy she raised. And I'm certain she would've been extremely proud of the man you've become."

He blinked, staring at her, struck silent.

"You're beautiful," she continued. "Your soul is so beautiful, and screw anyone who can't see it. Who refuses to see it."

"Mycah." He clasped her hips. To push her away, draw her closer, he didn't know.

"No." Her grip on him tightened. "I'm not finished. You're brilliant. You're scary brilliant. And I hope our baby has your brain." She brushed a kiss over his forehead. "Is the game finished yet? Have you shown it to anyone yet? Have you told your brothers about it?"

"It's almost done, and no." He shook his head, leaning back, releasing her. "Cain is a thorough man, so I can't imagine him not knowing about my past, but I haven't told either him or Kenan about the game—or me being in jail."

"Achilles." She sighed. "They would be your biggest supporters. If you would just let them. And I agree with you. Cain probably knows about your imprisonment. Which means he doesn't care and has accepted you anyway. Let them in."

Fear etched a jagged path through him. In spite of his resolve to keep them at arm's length, the two men had become important to him. He couldn't bear their rejection. But what if... What if they... Hope glinted underneath the doubt, the dread like a bright penny hidden in freshly turned dirt.

"It's a lucky person who you let in," she said, and he narrowed his gaze on her. At the note of—well, on another person, he would've called it wistfulness. "They must pass tests that make the ones in your video games look like child's play."

He cupped the back of her neck, drew her forward until their lips brushed. Until their breath mated. "Do you want in, Mycah?"

Uncertainty shifted in those mocha eyes, and her lips parted, moved, but no sound emerged. An ache, swift and sharp, sliced his chest but he smiled against her mouth.

"Better question, baby," he said, arranging her so she straddled him. "Do you want me inside you?"

A beat of hesitation, but she nodded, and he raised the short hem of her nightgown, balling it in one fist, revealing her pretty flesh to his greedy gaze. He lowered his hand between her spread thighs, spearing her folds with his fingers. In seconds, her wet heat bathed him, and they both groaned. She rode his hand, clutching his shoulders, her nails digging into his skin.

"Take me out," he ordered. "Take what you want."

She didn't hesitate this time. Quickly, she complied, and in seconds, she'd freed his cock and notched him at her entrance. Their gazes met, a silent question in her eyes, and he was sure the same occupied his. This was the first time they would have sex since she'd told him about the pregnancy. The damage, so to speak, had been done. They could go bare, and fuck, all he craved in this moment was to have her tight, hot sex squeeze him with nothing separating them.

But it had to be her decision, too.

She nodded. Again.

And it was all he needed.

With a groan that emanated from his gut—hell, his soul—he thrust high and deep inside her. And entered heaven.

And God help him, he never wanted to leave.

Fourteen

"So if you want to look through the presentation I emailed you later for more detail, you can. But to sum up—" Achilles set his tablet on the coffee table and propped his elbows on his thighs as he leaned forward and addressed Cain and Kenan "—Jacobi is a solid investment. It permits the client to manage backup and recovery through a single service. They have a full support team, and it removes the resource drain from the client as well as any significant time for training, leaving the client companies open to focus their attention on other matters."

"I'm just skimming through the presentation now—" Cain swiped over the screen of his own tablet, frown creasing his brow "—and I'll pass it on to Marketing and Legal, but I agree with you. And I trust your opinion. Kenan?"

"I looked it over before the meeting." His younger brother poured more coffee into his cup from the carafe in the center of the table. "Given you're the expert on this and not me, you still broke it down to make sense. The money saved in time alone would make the return on investment worth it. I'm going with your recommendation."

"That's settled, then." Cain set the tablet down on the table and picked up his own coffee. "Thanks, Achilles, I appreciate it."

"You're welcome. It wasn't a problem."

Shock suffused him. Shock and a warmth that originated from a place he couldn't quickly identify. Probably because he'd never experienced it.

Acceptance.

Trust.

These two men—who shared his DNA but were as different from him as cotton from silk—unconditionally trusted his opinion. Accepted *him*.

"One last thing, Achilles," Cain said, hesitating a beat. "Since you did the research and understand it and the company better than me or Kenan, would you feel comfortable presenting it at the next acquisitions meeting?" Before Achilles could answer, Cain set down his cup and held up a hand, palm out. "Don't feel pressured, but I believe you would be the best man for it."

"I'll do it."

Cain blinked and Kenan stared at him, both looking

as surprised as Achilles felt. Yeah, he hadn't expected to say that, either. But it was…right.

So was this leap of faith.

They would be your biggest supporters. If you would just let them… Let them in.

"Well, okay, then—" Cain smiled.

"If you two don't have anything scheduled and can give me a few minutes, I'd like to show you something."

Kenan shrugged a shoulder. "I'm free."

Cain studied him a long moment with that incisive stare. "Even if I did, I'd cancel it."

Another burst of that damn warmth. Throat tight, Achilles nodded and surged from the couch, grabbing his laptop bag. "Can I use your desk?"

Forty-five minutes later, he had his computer set up on Cain's desk, his program pulled up, and he'd explained everything about the video game—the setting, the target audience, the potential marketing…and the origination of the idea.

As he revealed his stint in prison neither Cain nor Kenan interrupted him, just let him relay his story until he completely finished.

And neither Cain nor Kenan looked shocked.

"You knew," Achilles flatly stated, not angry, not glad. Not… Hell, he didn't know how he felt.

"Of course I did," Cain said from his perch on the edge of the desk, arms crossed over his chest, no trace of remorse in his voice. "I had both of you investigated by the company's private investigator the moment after the will was read."

"And my father had you two investigated to rub in

my face the kind of men I'd abandoned Rhodes Realty to align myself with." Kenan smiled, but the amusement didn't reach his eyes. "You two are real reprobates, by the way." His lips twisted. "I fit right in."

"I'm a reformed reprobate," Cain drawled. "Love has changed me."

Achilles shrugged. "Three hots and a cot changed me."

"Great." Kenan scoffed. "What kind of brothers are you, leaving me out here being a degenerate on my own?" He shook his head, but the mock disgust melted away, and his scrutiny turned speculative. "So is the supposed 'jail secret' why you've kept your distance from us?"

Dammit. Leave it to Kenan to get to the awkward heart of the matter. Pinching the bridge of his nose, Achilles rose from Cain's chair and strode to the floor-to-ceiling window of the CEO office. His brother's office. Where he fit. Where he was born to rule. How did Achilles explain that to a man who knew from the cradle that he would be king?

He didn't know, but he had to try. Because the time for secrets, for remaining silent and shutting his brothers out, had passed.

Turning around, he met their identical gazes.

"When I received that letter telling me about Barron's death, I honestly don't know why I used that ticket. I hadn't thought of my so-called father in years. I didn't care about him—"

"Stop lying to yourself," Kenan interrupted softly. "You came to that will reading for the same reason I did. Because your whole life you felt something was missing. And you were hopeful that maybe, just maybe, you might find it."

Achilles parted his lips to object, to claim that his mother and grandmother had always been enough. But the denial wouldn't emerge. Because seeds of truth lay in that statement. Curiosity and, yes, hope had propelled him to get on that plane and come to Boston.

"Okay, I'll give you that. And I'll even give you that I found the something that had been missing my whole life. Brothers. But you're right. I have tried to keep my distance, tried not to become attached to either of you because after this year is up, I'm leaving Boston. I…" Even as he surveyed the luxury of the office, the paintings, furnishings, obvious signs of wealth and power, a small voice whispered—was it still true? With the baby, he hadn't allowed himself to think that far in advance. "I don't belong here. Not in Boston. Not in Farrell International. You two were born into this world. You know how to maneuver in it. You know its language, its rules. I don't. I love computers, codes, software, design. It's where I'm happiest, not negotiating contracts, closing deals, attending parties or learning how not to offend some person with how I talk or just being…me. This isn't my world."

"That's bullshit," Cain snarled, shoving off his desk and stalking over to Achilles. "The man who endured the childhood he did… The man who survived fucking jail and then forged a successful career for himself… The man who created that brilliant video game so youth like he once was can see themselves as courageous and heroic. That man will not run from some assholes who have nothing better to do than sit around, pick out napkins for their next dinner party and gossip about people who are too busy changing the goddamn world."

Cain got in Achilles's face, his frown fierce, fire burning in his gaze. "I know what it is to turn everyone away. To be alone and convince yourself that's what you want. That you're better off that way. I won't let you do it. Not while I'm here. I'll fight for you. Me. Kenan. Devon. You have family now. And we'll fight for you. You're not going anywhere. Not if I have to keep flying all the way across the country to that forest and camp outside that damn cabin until you give in and come home. Because *this is* your home now. Go visit the mountains to get away for a few days or weeks, but you come back. You're always going to come back to us. Goddammit."

Achilles stood there, rigid with tension, staring at Cain, who glared back at him. Both of their hands curled into fists at their sides, and out of his peripheral vision, he caught Kenan standing a couple of feet away, glancing back and forth. Probably waiting to see whom he would need to tackle first.

Inhaling a deep breath through his nose, Achilles nodded. "Okay."

Cain blinked. "Okay?"

"Wait, okay?" Kenan parroted.

"Yeah." Achilles exhaled and a weight lifted from his chest. A weight so heavy, he shouldn't have been able to breathe all of these years. "I'll stay."

A smile slowly spread across Cain's face. "Yeah. Okay."

"Well, just out of curiosity, what was it that convinced you?" Kenan propped his fists on his hips. "The 'we'll fight for you' or the 'goddammit'? Both were equally compelling."

"Never miss a good chance to shut up," Cain growled at Kenan before turning back to Achilles. "One more thing. Your video game. I don't know what your plans are for it as far as distribution, but I'd like to sit down and talk to you about it. Because I want Farrell to do it. And not just yours. But more like it. Matter of fact, I want you to do the research on either acquiring or founding a company specifically to design games with the mission and vision you described to us. And I want you to run it."

Achilles turned to look at his laptop, at the art, the game he'd been working on for a year but that had been in his head for nearly ten. And now he could be part of bringing to life more like them and putting them in the hands of millions of kids?

"Yes," he rasped. "I accept."

Cain clapped him on the shoulder, then pulled him into a tight hug. "Welcome home," he murmured into his ear.

"Does this mean you're finally going to leave the basement and take an office on this floor?" Kenan asked.

Achilles snorted. Then laughed. And it felt damn good.

"Come on, show me more of this game. And what

timeline are we looking at as far as getting it into beta testing. Can I be one of the betas?" Cain rubbed his hands together.

A chime echoed in the room, followed by a loud vibration. Frowning, Kenan removed his phone from his pants pocket. "Sorry, I need to check that. It's my notifications set to alert me if our name is mentioned in any..." He swept his thumb across the screen and tapped it a couple of times. His frown deepened as he scanned it, then his nostrils flared wide, his head jerking up. Eyes wide, he gaped at Cain. "Oh, shit, Cain."

"What?" Cain barked. "Kenan, what?"

"The society columns, gossip blogs, *Boston Noise* and the *Brahmin Post* are all publishing a story that Cain and Devon ended their engagement because he cheated on her and she found out."

"What the hell?" he demanded, his face darkening.

"That's not all," Kenan murmured. "They're all reporting Devon discovered you got another woman pregnant. Mycah Hill."

"Are you kidding me?" Cain thundered, stalking across the floor and tearing the phone out of Kenan's hand. "Where in the hell would they get this shit from?"

Shock spread through Achilles like frost on a windshield, dread curdling in his gut. Dread and suspicion. He didn't know how they could've found out about the pregnancy, but he had an idea where the story could've originated.

Achilles had promised Mycah he wouldn't tell Cain and Kenan about the baby, but with Cain facing the potential damage to his relationship with Devon and his reputation, he didn't have a choice.

"Cain, Kenan." He waited until he had his brothers' attention on him. "I have something to tell you."

Fifteen

Achilles stared at the penthouse elevator doors, waiting for them to open. The security guard had called minutes ago, informing him that Mycah had arrived asking to be let upstairs. He'd been expecting her since the story about her and Cain's supposed "love child" had leaked three hours earlier.

His brothers had taken the news about Mycah actually being pregnant and Achilles being the father better than he'd expected. And they'd even been happy for him. Hugged him. But they were still confused how Cain's name had ended up involved in the story instead of his. That part—his suspicions—he hadn't revealed and couldn't without talking to Mycah first. But he had promised to try to clear up the mess. And that meant convincing Mycah that they could no longer maintain this secret about the baby. Not if it meant that others would be hurt by it.

You'll find out if she's ashamed of you.

He briefly closed his eyes as the ding announcing the arrival of the elevator rang in the apartment.

He'd finally know if he'd been only a dirty secret for the woman he'd fallen in love with after all.

If he'd repeated a history he'd promised himself never to revisit.

If he'd given a woman his heart again only to be told it wasn't enough. That *he* wasn't enough.

Yes, he would have his answer.

The doors slid open, and Mycah rushed out of the elevator, and though he braced himself for what the next few minutes would bring between them, he soaked her in. The sensual explosion of curls that graced her shoulders and framed her beautiful face. The long, cream wool coat that opened over a dark purple sheath dress. The color reminded him of the one she'd worn the night they first met. And he tried not to let that strike him as an omen. Because he couldn't determine if it would be good or bad.

"Achilles." Breathless, her lovely mouth twisted down at the corners, her espresso eyes dark with worry, she crossed the floor to him. She slid her hands over his waist, clutching his hips and tipping her head back to gaze into his face. "I'm so sorry. God, I'm so sorry."

"What are you apologizing for?"

She frowned. At the question or his even tone, he couldn't tell, but her grip tightened on him. "Don't pretend we both don't know who's behind that story being leaked to the media," she said, voice grim. "Who else could it be but my parents? I don't know how they found out about the pregnancy, but it's them. Since I started at Farrell, they've been on me to cozy up to Cain. Maybe this is their twisted way of doing it, of forcing us together."

"If that's true, then you shouldn't be apologizing for them. These are their actions, and they need to own them. Not you." When would she get tired of doing it? Anger sparked inside him, but he tamped it down. That wasn't his battle to fight; he'd gladly wage it for her if he could, but he couldn't. "But their actions have put us in a difficult position. And now we have choices to make."

She stepped back, her arms dropping down by her sides, and he almost reached for her, demanding she put her hands back on him. Let him absorb her warmth. Let him touch her when he dropped this bomb on her. Because physical connection seemed to be all they had— at least for her.

"What do you mean?" Her gaze searched his face. "What else happened?"

"I was with Cain and Kenan when the story broke. I had to tell them about us and the pregnancy."

She exhaled, the gust of breath long and soft. Crossing an arm protectively over her stomach and palming her forehead with the other hand, she paced away from him, crossing the living room to the window. He followed at a slower gait, allowing her space and time.

"Okay," she said after a couple of minutes. "I pretty much expected it had to happen. Especially since Cain and Devon are directly affected by all of this. I'm just so sorry they were dragged into this mess."

"Mess?"

She pivoted, frustration suffusing her expression and voice. Waving a hand, she shook her head. "You know what I mean."

"Yes, I do. And you're right—this is a mess of our making. Because we've failed to be honest. With our families. Our coworkers. Each other. Ourselves."

"What are you saying, Achilles?" she whispered, the barest hint of panic in her tone. A flash in her eyes.

"I'm saying we can only build a future on truth. No more hiding, no more secrets. Because they have a way of crumbling and leaving people broken."

"Time." She splayed her fingers wide over her belly, and this time there was no mistaking the alarm in her voice. It darkened her eyes to near black. "You promised me time to reveal this how I needed to…"

"That was before a hatchet job about my brother fathering my child hit the fan," he growled, anger surging inside him, hot and possessive. The thought that people believed his baby belonged to Cain. That his brother had touched Mycah, put his mouth on her, seen what she looked like lost in pleasure… Dammit. He scrubbed a hand down his face, his beard abrading his palm. "Mycah, you can't hide your pregnancy any longer. It's impossible. And we have to address the misconception of Cain being the father. For him and Devon as well as for the reputation of the company."

"I know, I've thought about this," she said in a rush, the words piling up on each other. "I'll make a statement confirming the pregnancy and debunk the lie that Cain is the father."

"And when they ask who the father of the baby is? Because they will ask, Mycah." His body stilled, everything in him waiting for her answer.

"I'll tell them that information is between me and the father and we wish our privacy to be respected."

Pain, anger, sorrow, regret—they crowded into his chest, squatters claiming room and shoving against his rib cage for more space. They filled him, the pressure so great, he breathed the emotions, tasted them, became them.

"You do know not giving them a definitive answer will only flame the fire, not put it out, right?" he asked, surprised at how calm he sounded when a storm raged inside.

She shook her head, curls grazing her shoulders. "Not if we handle it correctly—"

"Are you that ashamed to admit that I'm the father of your baby?"

Her chin jerked back as if his accusation had delivered a verbal blow. Shock widened her eyes, parted her lips, and she blinked at him as if slow to comprehend his question.

"Achilles," she finally whispered, lifting an arm toward him and shifting forward. "That's not true. I could never—"

"Be embarrassed by me?" He arched an eyebrow, the corner of his mouth quirking. "Try again, Mycah. You forget, I've done this before. I'm familiar with the script. Intimately."

"I'm not her," she said, her fingers curling into her palm. "I'm *not* her."

"I know that. I've known that for a while. Doesn't mean history isn't repeating itself."

Accept me. Accept us.

"You're not being fair," she accused, and he hardened his heart at the desperation there. "The reasons I explained to you still stand. They're still valid. Even more so now that this story leaked the way it did. Which, I suspect, was part of my parents' reason for doing it. I'm unsure about my position with Farrell. Can Cain afford to keep me on with rumors of his supposed mistress working for him? And what about my professional reputation? Now more than ever I need to control the narrative and not allow them to steal that from me. To destroy years of hard work, to ruin how my coworkers and peers look at me. And while I haven't slept with Cain, if it comes out that I did sleep with the other CEO of the company, it would undo everything. I don't get a second chance at this. All I'm asking for is time, Achilles. You can't just flip the script because it's convenient."

"Convenient?" He stepped closer to her, then stopped. Getting nearer to her so he could inhale her scent, touch her—that was a mistake. Then…fuck it. He eliminated the distance between them, not stopping until his chest pressed to hers, his thighs bracketed hers. She tipped her head back, meeting his gaze. He ached to brush his fingertips over her elegant brows, those sharp cheekbones, that trembling, sensual mouth. But even he had his limits. "You're not the only one out on that limb, Mycah. I'm right there beside you. Fuck, I want to be there with you. Just like you told me to do with my brothers—let them in. Now I'm asking you. Let me in. *Let me, baby.* This—" he gave in, stroked a hand down her hair "—there's nothing convenient about this."

"Isn't it?" she asked softly, her eyes dark with shadows, heavy with sorrow. "And what happens when you decide that I'm not enough anymore? That I've disappointed you? What then? What will I have left? My baby and my career. You're leaving Boston, or have you forgotten that, too? I'll co-parent long-distance, and my career, it's the only thing I have complete control over. I sacrificed it before, for a man. And I nearly lost everything I worked so hard for. Nearly lost all trust in myself and who I was in the process. I'm not willing to do that again."

Achilles dropped his arm. Took a step back. Damn near stumbled as pain and grief punched a hole in his chest, his heart. For him, for her.

For whom they could've been.

"You have so little faith in me—in yourself."

A sense of futility swamped him, and instinctively he battled it, almost reaching for her, needing to hold her, make her see that if she'd just fight for him...

Love him.

He briefly closed his eyes and pressed his fist to his chest, rubbing the ache there. Her gaze dropped to the movement, and he stopped, walking past her to take her former place at the window, blindly staring out at the view that so many people would—and did—pay millions for.

And him? He'd give it all away to wake every day to her.

"It amazes me that you don't see in yourself what I do. What everyone else does. You've been at Farrell for a matter of weeks, and already you have the respect of those who work under you and who are over you. I'm not minimizing your concerns, but I am saying that you're not taking into account how fiercely people will go to bat for you because of their respect for your work ethic, your record and your character. And you as a person. You don't just change procedures and cultures in a company, Mycah, you change people. You changed me."

He turned, faced her. As the glutton for punishment he'd called himself before, he needed to look into her eyes for this.

"I arrived in Boston alone, closed off, mistrustful, bitter, angry and looking for the exit back to Washington. I'm still not what anyone would call a people person, but I have family now—brothers. And not just in name only. Brothers who I trust, who trust me, who I want to become closer to. Not only do they accept me but they want to support me. Like my game. Cain wants to fund it, distribute it."

"God, Achilles, that's wonderful," she breathed, delight for him briefly dispelling the shadows in her eyes. "I'm so happy for you."

"You gave that to me. Because you encouraged me to trust him and Kenan. I'm letting go of the past, of the hurts, the anger. And today, I told Cain I would stay in Boston." As shock flashed across her face and her fingers fluttered to the base of her throat, a faint smile curved his mouth. But without humor. "I might have said I would today, but truthfully? I'd made the decision when you told me you were pregnant. I couldn't be a part-time father. And by then, the thought of leaving had me sick inside. Because it meant leaving you. It meant leaving the woman I was falling in love with."

"Achilles," she whispered.

He shook his head, cutting her off. "This isn't for you, baby," he said. "It's for me. I love you. And yes, maybe I'm not being fair to lay this on you, either. But I'm not asking you to do anything with it since at this point, you don't believe you can—or you don't want to. I settled for a half relationship in secrecy once. I won't do it again. I want more. I want it all. Because I'm willing to offer you everything I have and am in return—a husband, a friend, a protector, a lover, a father to our baby. I deserve more than scraps of you."

He glanced away from her, from the stricken expression that damn near brought him to his knees.

"Achilles, you don't understand. Just give me—" She stretched a hand toward him, but when he stared at it, she slowly lowered her arm.

This was a matter of survival. And if she put that hand on him, he might not have the strength to do them both the favor of ending this before they hurt each other beyond repair. They still had to be parents to their baby.

"And then what, Mycah? Another month? Another excuse? I can't." He slid his hands into the pockets of his pants. "Please let me know when your next doctor's appointment is. We'll probably have to be more careful given the publicity with the story, but I won't be shut out. I still need to be part of the pregnancy."

She wound her arms around her torso, and after a moment, nodded. And after another longer moment, she turned and walked across the apartment, stepped into the elevator and left him.

How long he stood there, staring out the window, he didn't know. But when he did stir, the pain, the sorrow crushing his sternum, hadn't eased. Only this time, he didn't have to face it alone.

Removing his cell phone from his pocket, he dialed his brothers.

Sixteen

Mycah glanced up from blindly studying her computer screen when she heard the knock on her open office door. She forced a strained smile, waving Kenan Rhodes inside, although her stomach tightened, and it had nothing to do with morning sickness.

He returned the smile, closing the door behind him.

Her belly pitched harder.

If they were going to fire her, they would send the charmer to do it. Sugar with medicine and all that.

She should be worried about losing her job, but as she met his blue-gray gaze, all she could think about was another man with those eyes. A man she hadn't seen in two eternally long days and nights. A man she couldn't evict from her thoughts. A man who'd entered her life, ravaged it like a midnight storm and left her irrevocably altered.

He'd claimed she'd changed him.

No, Achilles had it wrong. He was the perfect storm. And her?

Apparently, a storm chaser.

But that was over. And she stood alone. Again. Shivering in the cold. By choice? Maybe. Yes. God, but it didn't feel like it. She'd just been trying to protect herself, protect her career. Was that so selfish?

Protect yourself?

Or hide behind your career?

She silently cursed at that annoying voice that wouldn't shut up—that had refused to shut up—these past two days.

"I just wanted to stop by and see how you're doing." Kenan dipped his head toward the visitor's chair in front of her desk, silently requesting permission to sit. She nodded, and he sank into it. "You did a great job at the press conference."

She grimaced at the mention of the short press conference the PR department arranged that morning to address the article. It'd been held in the lobby of the building. Mycah had made a short statement and had refused any questions.

"Thank you. It's a sad day when a businesswoman has to make a public statement about the status of her womb." She released a sound somewhere between disgust and relief. "I'm just glad it's over. At least that part of it. How are Cain and Devon doing?"

Kenan rolled his eyes, a smirk tugging the corner

of his mouth. "Disgustingly okay with going around exhibiting extra displays of public affection to dismiss rumors of his defection." He sobered, the smile fading from his lips. "They'll be fine. Neither one of them are strangers to public scrutiny. How are you doing? In the spirit of full disclosure, Cain and I spent the evening with Achilles a couple of nights ago."

A deep, bright ache bloomed in her chest, and she shifted her gaze from his, unable to look into those eyes any longer.

"How is he?" she rasped.

"Not good," he said bluntly. She whipped her head back toward him. "But he'll be okay."

"I suppose you and Cain resent me. I can't say that I blame you."

"For what? Giving Achilles a reason to stay here in Boston?" Kenan arched an eyebrow. "Cain might think he did that with his caveman 'You stay here' speech, but I know it was you. You and the baby. His love for you. You brought my brother to life. I could never resent you for that."

"I broke his heart," she whispered.

"Yes, you did."

"C'mon, Kenan." She leaned forward, her fingers curling into her palm. Her chest rose and fell on her elevated breaths. What game was he playing? Part of her wanted, *needed*, him to lash out at her. Punishment? "He had to tell you my reasons for not wanting to reveal he's the father of our baby just yet. Or why *he believes* I don't want to tell anyone."

"I understand what he believes. I also understand

your reasons." Kenan reclined in the chair, elbows propped on the arms, fingers steepled under his chin. "Mycah, do you watch football?"

She frowned, confused at the sudden switch in subject. "I live in Boston. Will saying no get me fired?"

"Possibly. Probably. So just plead the fifth. Anyway, nearly seventy percent of the NFL players are Black. But fewer than ten percent of the coaches are Black. And if one of those coaches are fired? It's almost impossible for them to acquire another coaching position in the league or even college. While if a white coach is let go, he might have two or three more jobs with different teams, just in the league alone."

He lowered his arms, his gaze bright, intense. For the first time since meeting the youngest Farrell brother, she glimpsed another side of him.

"The society we exist in isn't set up for minorities to win. And when we do make our own opportunities and lose them for some reason? Fail? That same system isn't set up for our recovery. It's different for the white male—and to an extent, the white woman—because they can fail, can come back for a second and third chance, and go even higher, achieve even more. But not us. We won't be the first rehired, and chances are slimmer that we'll achieve that pinnacle again within the same company. Is it any wonder we're in a constant dogfight where we battle like hell not to give in, never to fail because we know the odds of recovering aren't there? That if we're going to make it, we're going to have to do it outside a rigged system? So yes, Mycah, I get it." He nodded. "I get why you guard your career so fiercely. You're a Black woman who has a lot to lose." He paused, cocked his head, studied her for a long moment. "And if that's all there was to it, I would leave it alone. Because as a Black man in the same society, I'm the last person to stand in your way."

The relief from being *understood* chilled at his cryptic words. "What're you talking about, if that's all there was to it?"

His expression softened. "I meant it when I said we're from the same world, Mycah. Our families are... very similar." An emotion too quick to decipher flashed in his eyes. "Another thing Achilles can't really understand but I do. The responsibility toward them. And I may be a complete hypocrite right now, but you can't live your life for them. For an approval that is based on conditions. Because there will always be more conditions. Unachievable stipulations. Impossible goals. And you'll lose yourself trying to obtain them. And one day you'll wake up and realize that while they've been living their lives, yours has passed you by with nothing to show for it. Nothing but the reflection of someone else's dreams for you instead of your own."

"Yes," she said, fear, sadness and pain clogging her throat. Pressing against her chest. She briefly closed her eyes. "Yes."

That's all she could say and yet, it captured everything. Just as Kenan had.

Achilles believed she was ashamed of him. That she didn't want to tell her parents about the pregnancy because of that shame, and nothing could be further from the truth. She couldn't be more proud to have him as the father of her baby. There was no other man she wanted but him. The embarrassment belonged to her. Because as soon as she shared the news with her parents, they would use it…twist it. She harbored no doubts about that, about who they were. So she'd longed to keep this special news—their baby—between them for just a little while longer before she had no choice. Keep it pure and just theirs.

But her parents had managed to ruin it anyway.

No. The truth opened up inside her like a lamp clicking on, chasing away the darkness. No, she couldn't place all of this on them.

Because in the end, these were her choices, and the time had come to accept the truth and own those choices.

Yes, she'd worked all these years to establish a career she could be proud of, to provide for her family. But she also used both as a way to protect her heart from further hurt, to shield herself from rejection and the pain of being deemed unworthy, never good enough. While her parents had never said the words, while her employers had never written them on a review, the implications had always been that she'd had to work twice as hard, be twice as good… And she'd done everything to achieve a goal that would always be this dangling, golden carrot.

But Achilles… She huffed out a chuckle that ended on a soft sob.

Achilles had never asked her to be anyone but herself. He'd never asked her to decrease herself so he could be increased. He had loved her for herself—flaws and all. He'd worshipped those flaws, loved her *because* of them, not in spite of them. But she'd allowed her fears to prevent her from claiming him for herself even though she so desperately longed to.

Because she loved him.

God, she loved him.

And she was living in fear of rejection, of disapproval.

Of loss.

No matter the consequences of living in the light and out loud, she'd willingly face them. If that meant whisper campaigns from business colleagues, a hit to her reputation, ostracism from her family—so be it.

She was going to claim the life she wanted and finally, finally live it. And if he'd have her, she was going to claim the love of her life.

"So are we going to do this?" Kenan asked.

She startled, almost forgetting he still sat in the office with her. Glancing at him, she smiled.

"Oh, we are so doing this."

"Good." He clapped his hands together, rubbing them, a grin of what could be called only glee spreading across his handsome face. "Did I ever tell you how I single-handedly saved Cain and Devon's relationship? True story."

Seventeen

For what could possibly be the last time, Mycah climbed the front steps to her parents' home. Enough anger flowed through her that the thought of never entering the house again was okay with her. But underneath, the love for them that she could never eradicate made her hope it wouldn't be the final time she entered the place where she'd grown up. The last time she was with her parents.

But that would be their decision.

She used her key and let herself in, then removed it, setting it on the mantel. Odd not to have the key she'd had since she was twelve on her ring, but it was only the first of many changes in her life. Heading toward the rear of the house, she inhaled a deep breath to calm the nerves that fluttered against the walls of her stomach like a flock of migrating birds.

I can do this. I am *doing this.*

Because it needed to be done.

There was no going back.

She paused in the entryway to the small family room. As she'd expected, only her parents occupied the room; her father sat on the couch reading one of the murder mysteries he loved, while her mother commandeered the antique writing desk. At three o'clock, Angelique wouldn't arrive from school for another hour or so, depending on if she had play practice. Good. Because this wasn't a conversation her sister needed to overhear.

"Mom, Dad." Mycah entered the room.

"Well, this is a surprise." Her father set aside his book, smiling.

"It certainly is." Cherise rose from her chair and crossed the room to pull her into a hug, air-kissing both her cheeks. "A good one, though."

"Is it really?" Mycah asked. "You two should've expected me sooner or later."

"I don't know what you mean, honey." Her mother waved a hand, retracing her steps to lower to the couch next to Laurence. "Why don't you sit down, and I can—"

"No, that won't be necessary. I'm not staying long, and this isn't a social call."

"Mycah, interrupting your mother is unnecessary," Laurence admonished. "We didn't raise you to be rude."

"I hate to disappoint you, but I'm afraid that might become the norm, so you might need to become used to it." She cocked her head, coolly eyeing them. "Which one of you did it? Which one of you went to the media and told them I was pregnant?"

They didn't even have the grace to appear remorseful. Not even a little bit. If anything, annoyance crept across her mother's face. Annoyance that Mycah bothered her with this?

Jesus.

As if she didn't have the right to be angry.

"Is that what all this is about?" Cherise flicked a hand. "Neither one of us went to the media. I did happen to mention to Margaret Dansing that you were expecting while we were lunching. I'm not responsible for what she did with the information."

"Margaret Dansing. The same Margaret who told you about seeing me with Cain. The same Margaret whose daughter is a columnist with the *Brahmin Post*." Mycah seethed. Paused. And reminded herself this was her mother. She couldn't disrespect her even though, God knows, the woman couldn't give a damn about the word *respect* when it came to Mycah. "How did you find out?"

"Dr. Luther's office. The nurse there congratulated me on becoming a grandmother. Do you know the embarrassment you caused me when I had to pretend to know what she was talking about?" Cherise frowned. "Really, Mycah, I should've been the first person you told."

"Because of what you did with the information when you did find out?" she snapped. "How could you, Mom? Did you even care about the damage you did? To me?

To Cain and Devon? To Achilles? Did you even care that it wasn't Cain's baby? Or that people only believe it was. That's all that mattered to you."

"I didn't say who fathered it," she said calmly. "I let Margaret draw her own conclusions. And since she'd just seen you dining with Cain…" She shrugged a shoulder. "But yes, anyone else is better than people believing *that man* fathered *our* grandchild," she bit out. "What were you thinking, Mycah?"

"I wasn't thinking about you."

"That much is obvious," Laurence said, shaking his head. "What's done is done. And you still get to keep your little job because Cain couldn't very well fire the mother of his child and look good in the public eye. It all works out in the end and it's for the best, if you ask me."

"It's for the best?" She stared at them. Gaped. Good God. She loosed a disbelieving laugh. She'd been protecting them all this time when they were ready to sacrifice her—her happiness, her well-being, her future—for themselves. "The best for who? You? You're connected to the Farrells, but through the *right* Farrell. And I still work and support you with my 'little job.' Well, I hate to break it to you, but that ends here."

"What are you talking about now, Mycah?" Cherise asked, leaning forward and picking up a magazine off the table in front of her. "You're being so dramatic about this, but like I told you before, you'll see we've only ever wanted the best for you. Eventually, you'll understand that."

"Oh, I see more than you think now. My eyes are

wide open." She reached into her purse and withdrew a check she'd written out beforehand and set it on the table. "That's a check that should be enough to cover your household bills for three months. I'd spend it wisely because after it's gone, it's the last money you'll receive from me. I'm through supporting you."

"What are you talking about, young lady?" Her father surged from the couch, his book tumbling unheeded to the floor.

"Just what I said. I'm done. I'll continue to pay Angel's tuition and any of her needs because she doesn't deserve to be penalized, but the tuition will be paid directly to the school. As for you two, I suggest you actually start going into the Hill-Harper office or downsize or actually learn to live off a budget. Because I'm done allowing you to use me. This relationship is toxic, and I can no longer afford it—emotionally or financially. So you're cut off."

She turned and headed for the entrance to the family room, ignoring their indignant calling of her name. But at the last second, she pivoted, holding up her hand, palm out.

"One last thing. Achilles Farrell is going to be in my life. And not just as the father of my baby, but as my husband, if he'll have me. And if you can't accept that, then I'm sorry. I'm even sorrier that it's a decision you're making not to be in your grandchild's life. Because I won't have you disparaging my child's father. If you can't respect him, my choice of a husband and the father of my child, then you don't have to be a part of that family. It will sadden me, but again, that's your choice."

With that, she left and didn't look back.

She only looked forward.

Because only the future lay ahead.

Eighteen

"Is all this really necessary?"

Achilles scanned the huge office with the floor-to-ceiling windows, the sitting area with the dark brown couch, matching chairs, rug and coffee table. Black, glossy built-in cabinets surrounded a wide, flat-screen television on one wall, and a large, curving glass desk with a bank of computers that, admittedly, had him drooling, encompassed only half the space. There was plenty left for him to add whatever he wanted, because yes, this was *his* office.

On the executive floor.

He'd *finally* made the move.

But it wasn't the furniture, computers and amazing view that had him scowling at Kenan and Cain.

No, that honor belonged to the streamers, balloons, food and people crowded into the office.

"Yes, it's necessary. You're finally out of the basement and up here with your brothers. Now stop glaring at us. This is a no-glare zone," Kenan commanded, passing him a cup of—something red.

"Not to mention, you hired two people to help you work on your game and finish it. Think about that. You officially have the first two employees for your new company. Even before you have a name for it," Cain said, sipping from his own cup.

"I have a name for it." Achilles scrubbed a hand over his hair, then slid it in his pants pocket. "Farrell Brothers Incorporated."

Cain and Kenan stared at him. Then slow, wide smiles lit both of their faces.

"I love it." Cain nodded.

"It's fucking perfect," Kenan agreed. "Now you really have to drink up, because we have to toast to Farrell Brothers Inc."

Achilles lifted the cup—still didn't know what he was drinking—to his mouth when movement from the doorway caught his eye. He glanced up...and froze.

Mycah.

It'd been four days since she'd left his apartment, and fuck, it might as well as have been four months. Four years.

Or four minutes.

He missed her.

Like an amputated limb, she was gone—he knew she was gone—but he felt her phantom presence in the living room where they'd made love, in the bedroom where he'd told her about his past, in the kitchen where he'd fed her.

Because they were on different floors at work, it'd been easy to avoid her, and he hadn't attended the press conference. Hadn't watched it, either. As it was, when she'd emailed him the date of the doctor's appointment three weeks from now, he would need every day of that time to prepare himself to see her.

He hadn't been ready for four days.

God, she was beautiful.

In another one of those pantsuits that were both professional and sexy as hell. What would she wear when she started showing? Excitement and greed spiked inside his chest, low in his gut, because dammit, he wanted to know. Wanted to be there with her in the mornings when she dressed, to caress and hold her belly, wait for their baby's movements under his palm.

But she didn't want that.

At least not with him.

He drew back, mentally and physically.

Glancing around, he noted the looks thrown her way and heard an undercurrent of whispers. His gut tightened, and he remembered her worry about the hit to her reputation. Anger ignited within him. Yes, she'd broken his heart, but damn if she deserved this.

"Mycah." He held up a hand, waved her inside. "Come on in. Grab a plate and something to drink."

Relief flashed across her face, and she briefly smiled, stepping into the office. He spied the two gift boxes, one medium-sized and the other smaller, she carried as she neared, and his gaze flickered from the packages to her.

"I'm sorry to just drop in without…"

"Mycah, you don't need to apologize," he murmured. "Everyone's welcome."

"Right." An emotion that could've been hurt flickered in her eyes, but before he could ascertain it, she handed him the larger gift box. "For your office, and a belated gift for your new company."

Setting his cup down behind him, he accepted the present. For several seconds, he just held it, staring down at the gaily wrapped package. Finally, he lifted the top and pushed aside the tissue paper, revealing a framed picture.

No, concept art.

From his video game.

Speechless, the bottom part of the box dropped from his hand, unnoticed.

It wasn't one of the images he'd shown her, but something completely original that she must've had commissioned.

She'd plucked the vision straight out of his head. His teenage hero, wearing a hoodie, jeans and sneakers and bearing a shield and sword, stood on an inner-city street, the landscape of old buildings, cracked streets and dim shadows surrounding him. And in the distance, a dark castle, thick forest and maze.

He wrenched his gaze from the framed art to the woman in front of him.

"I commissioned it after you showed me your video game. I thought it would make great cover art for the game. But you're under no obligation to use it. I just wanted you to know I'm one hundred percent invested in your dreams—in you. And…" She sank her teeth into her bottom lip, and his fingers clenched around the frame, needing to thumb the sensual flesh free. "This is for you, too."

She handed him the second box.

"I'll hold that for you," Cain murmured, taking the art.

Reluctantly, he turned it over, his heart thudding in his chest as he accepted the smaller gift. He didn't hesitate this time to open the present. Lifting the top, he removed the tissue paper, and as he stared down at the tiny item nestled inside, shock and then joy exploded in his chest.

He picked up the yellow onesie and read the bright green stitching on it aloud. "My daddy makes heroes."

Around them, a couple of gasps and more murmurs filled the room before it fell into total silence. But he didn't care. All of his attention remained focused on her. The woman who had just announced in front of his brothers and an office full of employees that he was the father of their baby.

"I know I asked for time, but over the last few days I've realized that time can be our greatest gift…and our worst enemy. I don't want another day to go by with you believing that I'm ashamed to declare to whoever will listen that you're the man who will teach our child what it is to be strong, respected and good. You're the man who will raise our baby with me, guide him or her, show them what true character is, what kindness is. Show them what it is to be loved. Because you've shown their mother all of those things. And I'm sorry I ever let you doubt it. I've allowed fear to run my life for too long, and I want to step out on that limb with you. Please forgive me, Achilles."

"There's nothing to forgive." And there wasn't. Because he'd forgiven her as soon as she'd left the penthouse.

"Yes, there is. I hurt you. But, Achilles, if you offer me your heart again, I'll take care of it. These past few days—" she shook her head, spreading her hands wide, palms up "—they've been so empty because you haven't been in them. My job, my family—they're all important. But not more important than my love for you. The life I want to build with you and our baby. *Our* family. I love you. So much more than I thought it possible to love a person. I don't just want you in my life, I *need you*. And I would be proud to stand beside you, with you, and claim you as mine, to be claimed as yours. If you'll let me."

Before the last word finished, he swallowed it with his mouth, tasted it on his tongue. Once more, he crushed those curls in his fingers, having missed their rough silk texture almost as much as he missed the flavor of her, the perfect fit of her pressed against him.

"I never rescinded my heart, baby," he whispered against her lips. "It's always been yours."

She laughed, the sound a bit waterlogged, and he cherished it. Had never heard anything as special, as wonderful. Not even the spontaneous outbreak of applause around them. Or Kenan telling everyone to stop being creepy voyeurs.

Achilles leaned his head back, joining in the laughter, his chest light, heart free. For the first time in… years. His heart was free. Because it belonged to another.

It belonged to Mycah.

"Tell me again," she whispered, brushing her fingers through his beard, her eyes glistening.

He smiled, covering her belly and their child.

"I'm yours. And so is my heart."

* * * * *

Youngest brother Kenan Farrell is a carefree charmer and playboy…and secretly in love with his best friend.

Don't miss the next Billionaires of Boston novel, available January 2022!

WE HOPE YOU ENJOYED
THIS BOOK FROM
⊕ HARLEQUIN
DESIRE

*Luxury, scandal, desire—welcome to
the lives of the American elite.*

Be transported to the worlds of oil barons, family dynasties,
moguls and celebrities. Get ready for juicy plot twists,
delicious sensuality and intriguing scandal.

6 NEW BOOKS AVAILABLE EVERY MONTH!

#2827 RANCHER'S CHRISTMAS STORM
Gold Valley Vineyards • by Maisey Yates
Things have been tense since rancher Jericho Smith's most recent acquisition—Honey Cooper's family winery. What she thought was her inheritance now belongs to her brother's infuriatingly handsome best friend. But when they're forced together during a snowstorm, there's no escaping the heat between them...

#2828 BIDDING ON A TEXAN
Texas Cattleman's Club: Heir Apparent
by Barbara Dunlop
To save their families' reputations and fortunes, heiress Gina Edmonds and hardworking business owner Rafe Cortez-Williams reluctantly team up for a cowboy bachelor auction. Their time together reveals an undeniable attraction, but old secrets may derail everything they hope to build...

#2829 THE EX UPSTAIRS
Dynasties: The Carey Center • by Maureen Child
A decade ago, Henry Porter spent one hot night with Amanda Carey before parting on bad terms. They're both powerful executives now, and he's intentionally bought property she needs. To find out why, Amanda goes undercover as his new maid, only to be tempted by him again...

#2830 JUST A LITTLE MARRIED
Moonlight Ridge • by Reese Ryan
To claim her inheritance, philanthropist Riley George makes a marriage deal with the celebrity chef catering her gala, Travis Holloway—who's also her ex. Needing the capital for his family's resort, Travis agrees. It's strictly business until renewed sparks and long-held secrets threaten everything...

#2831 A VERY INTIMATE TAKEOVER
Devereaux Inc. • by LaQuette
Once looking to take him down, Trey Devereaux must now band together with rival Jeremiah Benton against an even larger corporate threat. But as tensions grow, so does the fire between them. When secrets come to light, can they save the company *and* their relationship?

#2832 WHAT HAPPENS AT CHRISTMAS...
Clashing Birthrights • by Yvonne Lindsay
As CEO Kristin Richmond recovers from a scandal that rocked her family's business, a new threat forces her to work with attorney Hudson Jones, who just happens to be the ex who left her brokenhearted. But Christmas brings people together...especially when there's chemistry!

my father gave it to you. About the fact that we're stuck together, but will never actually be together. And that's why I had to leave. I'm not an idiot, Jericho. I know that you and I are never going to... We're not going to fall in love and get married. We can hardly stand to be in the same room as each other.

"But I have wanted you since I understood what that meant. And I don't know what to do about it. Short of running away and having sex with someone else. That was my game plan. My game plan was to go off and have sex with another man. And that got thwarted. You were the one that picked me up. You're the one that I'm stuck here with in the snow. And I'm not going to claim that it's fate. Because I can feel myself twisting every single element of this except for the weather. The blizzard isn't my fault. But I'm making the choice to go ahead and offer...me."

"I..."

"If you're going to reject me, just don't do it horribly."

And then suddenly she found herself being tugged into his arms, the heat from his body more intense than the heat from the sauna, the roughness of his clothes a shock against her skin. And then his mouth crashed down on hers.

Don't miss what happens next in...
Rancher's Christmas Storm
by New York Times *bestselling author Maisey Yates!*

Available October 2021 wherever
Harlequin Desire books and ebooks are sold.

Harlequin.com

HDEXP0921

*Things have been tense since rancher Jericho Smith's
most recent acquisition—Honey Cooper's family winery.
What she thought was her inheritance now belongs
to her brother's ridiculously handsome best friend.
But when they're forced together during a snowstorm,
there's no escaping the heat between them...*

Read on for a sneak peek at
Rancher's Christmas Storm
by New York Times *bestselling author Maisey Yates!*

"Maybe you could stay." Her voice felt scratchy; she
felt scratchy. Her heart was pounding so hard she could
barely hear, and the steam filling up the room seemed to
swallow her voice.

But she could see Jericho's face. She could see the
tightness there. The intensity.

"Honey..."

"No. I just... Maybe this is the time to have a
conversation, actually. The one that we decided to have
later. Because I'm getting warm. I'm very warm."

"Put your robe back on."

"What if I don't want to?"

"Why not?"

"Because I want you. I already admitted to that. Why
do you think I'm so upset? All the time? About all the
women that you bring into the winery, about the fact that

Get 4 FREE REWARDS!

We'll send you 2 FREE Books plus 2 FREE Mystery Gifts.

Harlequin Desire books transport you to the world of the American elite with juicy plot twists, delicious sensuality and intriguing scandal.

FREE Value Over **$20**

**Don't miss the next book in the sexy
and irresistible Jackson Falls series by**

SYNITHIA WILLIAMS

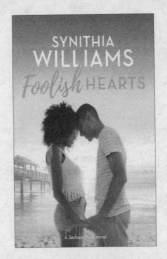

**There's nothing riskier than giving love
a second chance...**

"The perfect escape… Deeply felt, engrossing, soapy romance."
—*Entertainment Weekly* on *Forbidden Promises*

Order your copy today!

HQNBooks.com

PHSWBPA0821